COASTAL ELITE

KATE CANTERBARY

Always get lost
in Montauk ♡

kate
canterbary

VESPER PRESS

Copyright © 2017 by Kate Canterbary

Paperback ISBN 978-1-946352-03-3

Editing provided by Julia Ganis of JuliaEdits.
http://www.juliaedits.com/

Cover image by Lindee Robinson of Lindee Robinson Photography.
http://www.lindeerobinsonphotography.blogspot.com

Cover design by Anna Crosswell of Cover Couture.
http://www.bookcovercouture.com

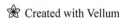 Created with Vellum

For the elitists, coastal and otherwise.

CHAPTER ONE

THE WORLD, IT WASN'T BLACK AND WHITE.

It wasn't a clean dichotomy of good and evil, right and wrong.

It was shades upon shades of gray, and I owned that gray.

And it was that gray which left me with little more reaction than an exasperated sigh when I found my girlfriend on her knees in my Capitol Riverfront apartment, sucking off my biggest competitor in the private military and security contracting industry.

One red-soled shoe was on the hardwood floor beside her, the other nearby, tangled in the straps of her Gucci purse. Her white-blonde hair had none of its usual precise styling, and that was all the proof I needed that she was working hard on the job at hand.

Most people would condemn Jocelyn. They'd call her a cheating whore. An evil bitch. A lying slut who couldn't keep her whoring and slutting out of my living room.

But me?

I didn't care enough to form an opinion. If I couldn't find the energy to care, then I couldn't exactly condemn her either. And there it was: the gray.

There was neither right nor wrong. No angels, no demons.

"Don't mind me," I said, slamming the door behind me.

"Kaisall," he—Toby Renner—boomed. He gestured to me in greeting as if this situation was both normal and appropriate for collegial conversation. It was neither. "What a pleasant surprise. Good to see you again, young man."

That anyone could articulate words beyond *yes*, *more*, *God*, and *don't stop* while on the receiving end of that kind of gratification was a crime. Either the offerings weren't good, or the goods weren't worth the offering.

And he was sure to tack on the *young man* quip. It wasn't about age but superiority. Renner stole it any way he could, even with his white briefs and khakis around his knees. His black polo shirt—emblazoned with his firm's ever-present and fully obnoxious spider logo—was stretched taut against his chest and arms, at least a size too small. It was all part of his gimmick, the shticky way he asserted his dominance without much to back it up.

I fucking hated the guy.

"As you were, sailor," I said, gritting my teeth.

Despite the shtick, Renner was one of the big dogs. He'd been in business since washing out of SEAL training—not everyone had the balls to make it through—but made a name on his ability to surround himself with the right people. He'd picked up major contracts during the wars in Iraq and Afghanistan, and beat me out for major protection details. He wasn't especially good at anything, but he gave plenty of people the impression that he was.

Based on the show in front of me, his dick followed that strategy, too.

I dropped my luggage from the past week's trip to the Middle East in the foyer without sparing another glimpse at Renner's pale ass and strode into my bedroom. Or, as much striding as a guy with titanium plates and rods in his leg could manage without affecting a pirate-styled limp.

There was no way in Satan's cozy hell that I'd limp in front of either of those cocksuckers right now.

Jocelyn was the kind of woman who dug in by inches. She started out as an entertaining fix-up who gradually claimed spots in every corner of my life until she was introducing herself as my fiancée. There'd been no ring, no bended knee, no popped question. By my math, that did not an engagement make, but she liked the *sound* of fiancée better, and I just didn't give a good shit. That, and she was talking about selling her Arlington, Virginia townhouse because she'd invited herself to move in while I was in

South Korea last month. I'd already asked her to pump the brakes on that one.

She could be my fake fiancée to her heart's content, but I drew the line at cohabitation. No sleep-overs here. I wasn't interested in that shit.

It wasn't like I'd been leading poor little Joss along either. I was loud and clear about my disinterest in anything involving the terms *serious*, *long term*, or *relationship*. None of that worked for me, and she'd insisted she was down for the same program.

Obviously, she was *not* down for that program.

But I hadn't been able to find the time to break things off with her. It was a dick move for me to have kept it going a minute longer than necessary, but she'd deserved better than an email or text. That, and I was somewhat certain she'd set fire to my suits if I dumped her while I was out of the country.

I was throwing clothes into a bag when Jocelyn poked her head inside. "About that—"

"Don't really want to hear the details, Joss," I said, grabbing a handful of boxers from the drawer. I'd never given any thought to another man's underwear, but right now I was really fucking pleased that Renner and I were on opposite sides of the boxers vs. briefs divide. "I only ask that you keep the semen off the rugs. That shit stains."

"Let me explain. It's not what you think," she said, sitting on the corner of my bed. Her lipstick was smudged and her mascara had run, but there wasn't an ounce of remorse in her expression. She was wearing one of those blouses, the kind that was nearly see-through and somehow office appropriate. She was like that, always playing her own shades of gray.

Working for the pharma lobby would do that to you.

"I'm not thinking about it at all," I said, shoving more clothes into the bag. I had no idea what I was packing, and it didn't matter. This only served as an outlet for my annoyance. "But it's time for you and Renner to get on out of here, yeah?"

"We got to talking one night, me and Toby," she said, her palms smoothing over her skirt. "And you've been traveling so much that—"

"Blowing him in my living room was the next logical step," I interrupted, my focus still on the duffel bag.

There were two possible explanations for this turn of events. One, Jocelyn was telling the truth and she happened to be cheating on me with an actual weasel. Or two, she was a pawn in another one of Renner's games and it was highly likely that he'd been pumping her for information about me and my business. Just another major fucking problem.

"You've been traveling for *weeks*," she said. "And even when you're home, you're busy."

"So you came here for a reminder?" I asked, shaking my head. Jocelyn hated my apartment (too small, too boring), and she wasn't one to be precious. She didn't cuddle up in my shirts or clutch my pillows. "Yeah. I get it, Joss. Now head on out."

She took a deep breath. "I was here to collect some of my things. I knew you were due back today, and I wrote you a note explaining that I needed to move on," she said. "And you've made it abundantly clear that you're not looking for anything serious."

I shook my head at the duffel bag. I was no relationship expert, but there had to be some ground between 'not looking for anything serious' and 'blowing a dude in your boyfriend's apartment.' Had to be. "Leave, Jocelyn. Now."

She sighed and muttered something under her breath that sounded an awful lot like *If that's how you're going to be* as she pushed off the bed. For a good long second, I thought about following her from the bedroom and beating the piss out of Renner. Just laying him the fuck out and feeding him his teeth.

But that was more effort than I was prepared to offer this situation, and I didn't need to send Renner off with the kind of busted-up face that would give him an opening to tell war stories all over Washington. And, more than that, I didn't make a habit of solving problems with fists. Too much of my work involved real danger and violence, and I didn't want that shit spilling over into my home.

There was a muffled discussion in the living room before the door snicked shut.

Fucking finally.

I released a rough, angry groan as my fingers curled into fists. The bag was out of my hands and flying toward the wall of Capitol Hill-facing windows before the sound fully left my throat, raining black and blue underwear across the room as it sailed.

Then I was panting, my heart pounding and chest heaving with the cumulative aggravation of this week. It was one fucking disaster after another —a large-scale rescue mission in Venezuela gone bad, resignations from five of my best field operatives, a dead-end pitch meeting in Riyadh, and now...*this*.

I yanked my phone from my pocket, and then whipped off my belt. I kicked my trousers to the corner—my poor cleaning lady was going to have her hands full this week—and stabbed the speakerphone button. Tinny ringing filled the room, mimicking the rush of pain in my leg while I pawed through the drawers in the adjoining bathroom. I flipped on the faucet when the call picked up. A little homespun interference for the digital age.

"Redtop Securities, this is Trish," sang a sweet, Southern voice.

"I need my apartment swept. The Montana protocol," I barked. The tube of prescription-strength numbing cream came into sight, and I slathered it from shin to thigh. "Lock down the servers. Re-encrypt all the comms, and use the heaviest layers we've got ready. Reset all the access codes. Switch out the locks, too."

"On it," she replied. The click of fingernails on the keyboard tinkled through the line.

"And pull the phone records for Jocelyn Gunderson," I said, leaning against the vanity. "Emails, too. Anything interesting, send it."

"You got it, boss," she said. There was a pause, her requisite sip of Diet Coke. In a can, with a straw. Always. "The team will be at your apartment within twenty minutes, and you'll have a data file with the information requested by end of day. Surveillance wants to know if you'd like to keep eyes on her."

"Yeah," I said, the word whooshing out as the ache in my leg eased. "But they should know she's in bed with Renner from Stillhouse."

"What a small, incestuous little world y'all live in," she said. Another slug of Diet Coke. "I can't say I'm disappointed to hear that because it means she's out of your bed. Right? Tell me this isn't some modern day time-share relationship, Jordan. I'll try, but don't think I can support that type of arrangement."

"No, Mom," I said, laughing for the first time in approximately six days. My mother had a way of doing that. She could always turn down the volume on terrible situations, and find new reasons to smile. If for no other reason than that, she was my most valuable employee. "I'm not sharing Jocelyn with Toby Renner. He can have her."

"Well, that's a blessing," she drawled. "How'd things turn out in Riyadh?"

"I don't want to talk about her anymore, and I'm in no mood to talk about Riyadh either," I said. "How are things? Did you hold down the fort?"

Her nails tapped against the keyboard again, and

then the soda can. "Nothing new to report," she said. "Will can fill you in on all the finer details. He's been in the weeds with Venezuela, and beating his little black book to death to line up some new staffing. Wait. Do y'all still have little black books?"

I laughed as I considered this. My business partner and mission commander, Captain Will Halsted, probably did keep his contacts in a black book. He was old-fashioned in obscure ways.

"Nevermind," she said before I could respond. "My age is showing. You're still meeting up with Will in the Hamptons, right?"

I pivoted, planting my face in the towels hanging from the back of the bathroom door, and groan-cursed into them. Joining Will and his family in Montauk as scheduled sounded like just the thing I needed, and if I left right now, I could be there before sunset.

But...there was work to be done. Mountains of it, especially after walking into this shitshow. I couldn't stop combing my mind for any bits of business I'd shared with Jocelyn, even the barest details. There wasn't much, but enough for Renner to go hogwild.

"I'd been planning on it, but I should get back to the office," I said.

She hummed and clucked for a moment, and then polished off the Diet Coke. That was my mother's subtle way of calling bullshit.

I scowled at my dive watch. It was five minutes before noon on Wednesday during the slow, humid part of summer when everyone colluded to get the fuck out of Washington, D.C. August in the Beltway was a swamp-ass misery, and I knew all about summertime misery. I grew up in the Mississippi Delta *without air conditioning* and spent two years in Afghanistan before receiving my honorable discharge from the Navy. I could handle heat. It was everything else that was giving me trouble.

"When's my next meeting?"

She cracked open another can, and then said, "You're due in Corpus Christi on Tuesday evening for a private dinner meeting with State Representative Rang Brattis at his country club. He'd like full service security for his home, land, and family as he gears up for a U.S. Senate campaign."

These guys. Seriously. They all thought there was a price on their heads. Big prices, too. That their coiffed wives and sweet, virginal daughters were one charity event or photo op away from being abducted and sold to the highest bidders. I'd come to realize it wasn't that they had an irrational fear of assassins or terrorists, but that they had something that required safe keeping. Whether it be information or business dealings or questionable relationships, they knew something dangerous could leak out. That was why they never blinked before agreeing to my terms and fees.

"Fuck it," I murmured. If the world was falling apart this weekend, I wasn't going to be the one putting it back together. Not this time. "Keep my calendar clear until after Texas."

"Jordan Elijah Kaisall," she seethed. "I don't care how old you are, you don't speak to me with that mouth."

"Yes, ma'am," I replied automatically.

Mama Trish wasn't particularly religious, but she was a big fan of phrases like *oh, sugar* and *cheese and rice* and *jeepers*. She did not swear. There was one time when I was in grade school when she'd closed her fingertip in the car door and yelled *Fudgy nuts!* but that was the closest thing to profanity I'd ever heard from her.

She took another pull from her soda, then huffed out a breath. "Your calendar is blocked."

There was a knock at the door, and I knew it was one of my tactical teams. When I wasn't setting up white-glove protection gigs for politicians and businesspeople, I was taking on government contracts. Mostly covert, mostly situations that never made their way to the newspapers, mostly so deep into those shades of gray that white and black were barely a memory. These guys shone in that type of work. They found needles in haystacks, and then quietly destroyed the needles. Or they took a shit-ton of needles and convinced the world it was a haystack.

Either way, they were talented as hell.

"The crew is here. I'm gonna go out to Montauk. Maybe Will and I can figure out some of this sh— sugar," I said. I didn't want to be here for this. I'd bet anything that Renner had left a data transmission bug of some sort, and I didn't want to regret letting him go without rearranging his face. He played dirty like that, dirtier than anyone else in the business. "Call me if you need me."

"Wait a flaming second," she said. "You're not driving to Montauk now. Not after spending the past eighteen hours on a flight from Saudi Arabia. Your knee—"

"It's fine," I interrupted, yanking on a pair of shorts. It was a bizarre style choice—cargo shorts, dress shirt, tie—but these guys didn't care. They wouldn't bother blinking twice if I was bare-ass naked. I switched off the speakerphone and opened the door for the team. "I'm fine. My leg is great. Do you have any plans this weekend? Are you seeing that dude Marco again?"

There was a thorough background check waiting at the top of my inbox about her newest beau. I wanted my mother to be happy and she definitely deserved to enjoy herself after raising my punk ass on her own and helping me start this business almost fifteen years ago, but I fucking *hated* these online dating sites. Holy hell. There was one week last year when she had four dates with four different men. Seven days, four dates. I didn't know anyone—man or woman—with that kind of game. I had to assign one of my analysts to full-time monitoring of her suitors.

She sighed. "You push yourself too hard, Jordan," she said softly. "I'd like you to slow down, and take a deep breath. Take a day off. Maybe even two days. You're allowed to do that, you know."

"I know, Mom," I said, leaning against the kitchen island. "Now, about this Marco—"

"Would you stop it? I'm not talking about dating with my son. I already know that you pulled a profile for him, so you have all the information you need right there." She paused, sipping her soda. "Did you think the data boys weren't going to tell me that you had him investigated?"

There was no possible way for this week to get worse. Especially not now that I had to remind some of the assholes working for me what *covert* meant.

"Try to have some fun this weekend, Jordan. Do you remember what that is? Fun? Where you do entertaining things and not look at your phone all the time?"

"Vaguely," I said. My rendition of fun involved trading insults with Will, or swimming five miles at the gym each morning, or eating bacon at every meal.

At the same moment, one of my techs held up a dime-sized electrode, the kind used to transmit extensive amounts of data, and said, "Got a live one, but it's got sisters."

Fuck this week.

CHAPTER TWO

BACK IN MY SEAL DAYS—BEFORE INTERNET streaming and satellite television were readily available—my unit watched *The Bachelor* as a matter of routine. We called it a hazing ritual for the new guys, but it was entertaining in a check-out-that-hot-mess kind of way. Exhausting days of training and rehearsal lived between the missions, and rose ceremonies dominated our dog-tired nights. Being SEALs, we couldn't simply enjoy the commercialization of modern mating rituals, and it was too easy to add some challenge to our viewing.

Shots every time a woman claimed another wasn't "here for the right reasons." Every time a hot tub was illogically integrated into the date. Every time the bachelor was filmed staring off into the distance, ruminating on his women while casually shirtless.

I'd been in Montauk for three hours, and this long

weekend already had the makings of an epic drinking game.

In this tonight's iteration of the game, I was drinking every time my business partner pawed at his wife or not-so-quietly whispered something suggestive in her ear. Or every time he tickled his baby daughter's belly and sent her into fits of giggles. Or every time he pressed me on the meetings I took in Riyadh, the details on those out-of-the-blue resignations, or anything related to Venezuela.

Drink, drink, drink.

My glass was halfway to my mouth—scotch with a chunk of ice because room temperature liquid reminded me of deployment, and not in the nostalgic way—when Will cleared his throat.

"About that meeting," he said, his daughter Abby snuggled on his chest. "Do you plan on filling me in, or should I wait for the official memo?"

I ran my hand over the back of my neck. "They weren't sold," I said. "Ultimately, they want us to jump through hoops for the contract. Make us sweat for it."

"Well," he started, his hands lifting and falling, "fuck that."

"I would, but—"

"No," he said. "*Fuck that.* We have more than enough work. We don't need to bend over backward for a shitty oil field gig that may or may not turn into a long-term asset protection detail. Our teams are too talented for that kind of horseshit. Fuck. That."

"Shitty," I repeated, "but spendy."

"We don't need the money," Will said. "We can expand our training facility in Maryland without it, Kaisall. You know that. You fuckin' know it."

That was where Will Halsted and I differed. We'd come up in the SEAL Teams together, deployed together, and now owned this company together, but our backgrounds couldn't have been more different. He was from sunny Southern California, and had a career military father, sweet-and-spunky mom, and two younger siblings. He was married to the love of his life.

I had none of that.

I grew up in northwestern Mississippi, painfully poor and lonely. Me and Mom, we moved around a lot. I could remember at least seven different apartments, and that didn't include the times we'd stayed in a spare bedroom or garage. Mom did the best she could, but I drank milk by the gallon, ate two pounds of turkey breast for lunch, and outgrew of shoes every three months until leveling off in high school. I hadn't made things easy on her.

I never knew my father. For many years, I'd peppered my mother with questions about him, as well as the occasional suggestion that I'd been adopted. In my mind, it'd been the only explanation that made sense, considering she was fair and blonde, and a tiny little thing, and I was five feet tall before starting the second grade. My hair was jet black, my eyes nearly as dark, and I'd been the first freshman in my high school's football history to take the field as a starting tight end. That I was even related to my mother had seemed unlikely.

I'd pestered her about my father without mercy, and the details leaked out over time. He'd played high school football. He was several years older than her, and their parents hadn't approved. He was Choctaw Indian, and I was the spitting image of him.

When I was an irritable teenager determined to resist all authority, I'd sworn to my mother that I would find my father and live with him instead of putting up with her outrageous rules. That was when she explained that he'd fought in the first Gulf War, and never returned. She'd only learned of his death when she caught sight of his picture on the front page of the local paper, and read about his military burial at Arlington National Cemetery.

I hadn't grown up with any expectation of security or stability. I didn't rest. I didn't know how, and I didn't believe I could or should.

Sure, Mom had a nice little place on the Gulf Coast now and she didn't work three jobs just to keep a roof over our heads or clothes on my back, but I didn't know to slow down. I'd hustled too long, and fuck if I knew what tomorrow would bring.

"I'll do the jumping," I said. It still stung that we were being asked to audition for basic work when we were one of the most skilled shops in the business. We were rarely asked for extended proposals. We didn't have to, not when our reputation preceded us. "I can handle the hoops. You stay in your command center, and go on playing *Call of Duty* all day."

Instead of working from our main offices in the Beltway, Will lived outside Boston. The arrangement suited us, somewhat to my surprise. I didn't know how to manage all the moving pieces without being in the thick of it and I didn't think I'd want to try, but Will required none of that. He pulled the strings on dozens of concurrent protection details, military support operations, and covert missions, and did it all from a tricked-out home office.

He stared at me for a long beat before rolling his eyes. "You're a fucking asshole, Kaisall."

It was true. The asshole part, not the *CoD* part. He was the best operator I'd ever met, and that I'd convinced him to join this venture with me was still a wonder.

"Don't you have better things to do?" he asked. "Rustle up other business. *Better* business. I can think of a handful of international NGOs and embassies that need bug-out plans, and covert-op-trained guys to pull them off the next time shit turns sour."

"And now you're telling me how to pitch? You want to move to D.C. too? Maybe sit in on some Senate Armed Services Committee hearings, or take meetings at the Farm? Oh, yeah, the CIA would be thrilled to have you on site," I said with a scoff. Will couldn't go anywhere in the military and intelligence communities without telling someone how to do their job. "Thanks. I got it."

Will patted Abby's back for a few moments, his brows pinched in thought. "Where's Jocelyn this weekend?"

I rocked back in my patio chair, groaning at the evening sky. "Marriage has turned you into a chick," I said. "Have we *ever* talked about women before?"

"Now that was a strong response," Will murmured. "A whole lot of protest when an easy answer would have sufficed."

"It was proportional," I said, mostly to myself. "Jocelyn is no longer."

"'No longer' meaning you're not together or you called in the wet team?"

"I didn't *kill* her, you asshole," I said. I couldn't say the thought hadn't crossed my mind once or twice since the crew had unearthed nine surveillance devices in my apartment. But she still wasn't worth that kind of effort. "It's over with her."

"Thank fuck," Will shouted.

The baby startled at that. He stood, and started pacing the patio, bouncing and rocking as he walked in the way that must come naturally to parents. "She was an obnoxious bag of silicone."

"They're real," I muttered halfheartedly. I didn't care whether Will thought her breasts were artificially enhanced, and I didn't care about Jocelyn enough to defend her honor.

"Oh, they're fucking not," Will replied. "She has the fakest tits I've ever—"

"That you've what?" Will's wife, Shannon, asked

from the patio door. She was four months pregnant, and had forced me to feel the baby kicking after dinner. It was a pleasant kind of strange. She was trying to recruit me to her side—she was betting this baby was a boy while Will disagreed—but I couldn't imagine making that kind of determination based on some kicks. "I'd like to hear the rest of this."

Unfazed by his wife's questions, Will said, "Jocelyn," and Shannon vigorously nodded in agreement.

"Completely fake. Collagen in her lips and cheeks, too. Oh, and all of her personality. Filled with plastic," Shannon said.

"Great. Nothing was real," I said, indulging in some self-pity. "She was gargling Toby Renner's balls when I got home from Riyadh. He doesn't mind the plastic."

Will stopped pacing. "Wait a minute. *What*?" he asked. "You've been here for hours and not once mentioned a word about Renner or Titsy O'Silicone."

I yawned, the weight of a week on the road settling down on my shoulders. Maybe it was age, maybe it was stress, but the physical demands of pinging around the globe only increased with each trip. Or maybe I was a walking version of Neil Young's "Old Man."

"I mentioned it just now," I said.

"But you didn't mention it *before*," Will said.

"Because I mentioned it now," I replied. Another yawn. My place was only two doors down from the beachfront home the Halsted clan was renting in the

Ditch Plains section of Montauk, but I was ready to curl up with Will's dogs and call it a night. That was a far better option than reporting that I'd been compromised. I wasn't ready to talk about that yet, not until I knew more. "Pardon me for not wanting to revisit that issue over dinner."

"I fucking hate that guy," Will said.

"No disagreement," I said, raising my glass. It was empty, but that wasn't going to stop me from toasting our shared loathing of Toby Renner.

"Let me ask you this," Will said. "Was he wearing the Stillhouse hat or polo shirt? Because you know he can't leave the house without one or the other. Or both." He turned to Shannon. "This asshole is notorious for wearing Stillhouse-branded shit in the middle of foreign conflicts and actual fucking war zones. He's got a damn target on his head and over his heart."

"And how is he still alive?" she asked. "Or in business?"

"Those are the great mysteries, Shannon," I murmured. "But it was the polo shirt today, Halsted. Extra tight." I flexed my biceps. "You know how it is, man. Gotta show off the guns."

"I fucking hate that guy," he repeated.

"Yeah," I replied. "But you didn't have to see his bare ass or watch Joss grabbing his sac."

Will shook his head and filled my scotch right up to the top. "That's brutal," he said.

"I'm sorry about all of this, Jordan," Shannon said,

rubbing my shoulder. "But things went well in Riyadh, right?"

Drink, drink, drink.

CHAPTER THREE

THIS OCEANFRONT COTTAGE—YOU COULDN'T CALL nine hundred square feet a house—was a splurge. An impulse buy after closing a huge deal with the Department of Defense a handful of years ago. My mother's house was already bought and paid for at that point, and she had a red VW Bug—her choice—and she'd ordered me to give myself something nice.

So I gave myself a beach cottage, even though I knew nothing about the Hamptons and surfing wasn't on my list of orthopedic surgeon-approved activities. In fact, I'd been flat-out forbidden from getting on a board again.

But it was a hobby acquired during my SEAL training on Coronado Island, and I wasn't entirely pleased with being told I couldn't do something.

It was that, coupled with my inability to sleep past sunrise, that had me up and rustling in the back shed for my longboard. The morning was young and the tide wasn't quite right for surfing, but I reasoned that I could at least paddle out. The beach was empty save for the joggers and dog walkers, and if I did nothing more than tread water and then head for the shore, no one would be the wiser.

The water was cold, colder than I'd expected for a humid August morning, but it was better than anything I'd felt in weeks. Like the stress and the shit were washed away, and all that remained was the lullaby of the ocean. Nothing seemed insurmountable out here, not even the list of issues and betrayals waiting for me on the other side of this weekend.

After finding a calm spot to watch the waves, I climbed up and straddled my board. The water was hypnotic, and if I didn't think too hard about my restrictions, this was almost as good as riding waves. I reached for my leg, feeling the lines and divots that ran from thigh to shin.

It only took two bullets to end my SEAL career. One from a machine gun pressed to the backside of my knee, and one from a rifle that left my tibial plateau in nineteen pieces. To say the mission had gone tits up would be an understatement, but there were silver linings. It ached every day, and it was really fucking ugly, but I'd survived and hadn't lost my leg. I'd deal with all the pain in the world to be alive.

Those silver linings were enough to minimize every restriction under the sun, and I slapped the water. "Fuck this shit," I announced, leaning forward to paddle into prime wave-catching position. "One ride won't kill me."

For several glorious minutes, that conviction held true. Everything was perfect...until it wasn't.

As the wave crested and I neared the shore, my front leg wobbled and slipped to the side. In attempting to recover, I overcompensated with my back leg. The pain was immediate, and I lost all control. I was thrown from the board, and plunged into the water. The board followed, pummeling me over and over as the wave crashed and churned toward the shore.

I swallowed more than my share of the sea before coming to the surface, but it was nothing in comparison to the fire pulsing through my leg. It wasn't the old familiar pain that I knew as clearly as my name and rank, but the fierce, searing twist of muscle and bone raging against metal. It was the type of pain that silenced my senses and narrowed my needs to escaping this torture. I'd been trained to ignore discomfort and physical limitations, but my worst, most grueling days in BUD/S were no match for this.

I dragged my sorry ass out of the ocean and flopped down on the sand, breathless and gagging and battered in both body and spirit.

I had to be reaching my lifetime maximum on shitty situations.

"Is everything okay here?"

I blinked at the sky several times before turning my head in the direction of the gentle voice. A woman's voice. There was no accent—New Yorker, Hamptons, or otherwise—but there was a kindness that my years of experience and business dealings told me couldn't be affected.

"Outstanding," I said. My jaw was locked and the word came out in broken grunts. It took a full minute to gather the energy to turn my head and face this woman.

Her eyes were full of sympathy—I *hated* the shit out of sympathy—and she dropped the mesh seashell bag she was carrying to the sand. "I'm not too sure I believe that," she said. Her brows crinkled as she approached me. "You had a pretty epic fall out there, and I think your board took a few whacks at you in the process. I wouldn't be outstanding if I'd been through that."

I was a breath away from writhing into the fetal position right there on the sand, and I probably would've yelped and howled if it weren't for the pretty dark-haired girl beside me. It really would've been easier if a burly guy with a sweater of back hair and ill-fitting Speedo had been the one to find my pathetic carcass.

I sucked in a breath and blinked away as much pain as my mind would erase. "Just a muscle spasm," I said.

Her gaze winged between my eyes and the hold I had on my knee, back and forth, back and forth. Her lips thinned, and then she sighed, muttering something to herself as she dropped beside me. She held her palms out over my leg, and shot a questioning glance at me.

"I'll just take a look. If that's okay," she said. "I'm an acupuncturist."

"Oh," I said, not sure what I thought about any of this. I didn't enjoy beautiful women seeing me in this condition. And she *was* beautiful, but it wasn't as much about her appearance as her nature. I wouldn't go so far as to call it something like her aura, but she had a vibe that felt right. I knew all about sugar-coated shit, and this woman was anything but. "Acupuncture. Right."

"Have you tried it?" she asked. Her fingertips met my skin, and I was too wrapped up in my misery to process her touch as anything other than awful.

"No," I said, the word morphing into a long snarl as I fought through the pain.

She traced the thick, leathery surgical lines on my quad, the ones that marked the locations of the rods and screws that held me together. "How old?" she asked.

I was thirty-nine, but that wasn't what she was asking. "Fourteen years," I said.

She pressed her thumbs to the outside of my knee and the white-hot pain almost had me springing off the sand.

"A lot of pressure built up here," she murmured. "You need to release this, or it's going to get much worse."

"You don't fuckin' say," I muttered, gasping and groaning through each word.

She continued pushing against my skin, some touches light, some much harder, but after several quiet minutes, the agony that had dominated every one of my senses was easing. The relief was nearly confusing, as if I'd grown so accustomed to the pain that I couldn't reconcile its absence.

"Better?" she asked.

I didn't answer. I didn't think I could speak without an assortment of gratitude bubbling over. I'd spent years chasing down remedies without real success, and she brought me relief with fifteen minutes of well coordinated poking.

She flattened her palm to my chest. "Breathe. Blow that tension out. Cleansing breaths, okay?"

I did, and repeated the process as she nodded in encouragement.

"Yeah, that's better," I said eventually.

She bobbed her head, her gaze still trained on my leg. "This is a temporary fix. You need to come by my place for some treatments," she said, lifting her chin toward the village. "I'm free tonight. Eight-ish. If you think my fingers are good, wait until I get my pins in you."

I sat up, wincing as I dug my heels into the sand. Oh, yeah. The pain hadn't left town completely. "Fuck," I seethed. "*Fuck*."

Her hand settled on my shoulder, right above my

SEAL unit's frog skeleton tattoo, and she squeezed. "I also do massage and Reiki—"

"Only in Montauk," I interrupted. The world beyond Clarksdale, Mississippi was big...and indescribably eccentric.

She laughed at that, and nodded as if she understood the oddness of this town. The gray-shingled mansions and the beach shacks. The posh village and the humble local hideouts. The boomtown summers and the ghost town winters.

"Look, I know big, tough guys like you probably don't buy into holistic approaches, but I can promise to ease some of the discomfort you're feeling. Even if it sounds like voodoo."

"The Veterans Administration hasn't taken up voodoo yet," I said, laughing.

She shrugged as she brushed the sand off my bare shoulder. "I get that. Most people have some preconceived notions when they come in, and some never find the balls to come in at all," she said. She offered a warm smile. "If you have the balls, I can promise it's not voodoo."

It was one of those smiles that didn't live in her lips but her eyes. It was more genuine than any bright, teeth-baring grin. And she really was pretty. Dark coffee eyes that matched her dark hair, and light olive skin beneath her t-shirt and running shorts. More than a few curves in all the right places. She was young but not *too young*. Early thirties, but I was certain she wasn't a day over thirty-five.

But then again—what the fuck did I know? I'd been laboring under the assumption Jocelyn's rack was real until last night. Look where those instincts got me.

"Do you know the bakery?" she asked. "Seashore Sweets?"

I pointed to my abs. My trainer was paid good money to keep them washboard quality. "Does it look like I eat many cupcakes? I may be laid out like a starfish here, but I'm not—"

"Down, boy," she said, patting my back. Her touch, it was pleasant. Easy and confident, and lingering a little too long to be chaste. "Everyone in town knows the bakery. Even the cupcake deniers."

She was right about that. You couldn't miss the hot pink seashell painted on the storefront window, or the smell of cake wafting through the village when the wind was right.

"I live in the loft above the bakery," she continued. "Stairs around back. Come up any time after eight."

I thought about this for a second. "Pins, huh?"

"You can handle it, big guy," she said, her gaze swinging from my shoulders to my toes. It didn't feel sympathetic this time. It felt like an appraisal, and a good one at that.

"Hey. Kaisall."

I glanced over my shoulder and found Will marching toward us through the white sand, his surfboard tucked under his arm. She looked at him, and then back at me.

"Above the bakery," she repeated. "If you can handle a few pricks."

She popped up and grabbed her seashell bag, winking as I watched her. Like I could leave that challenge unacknowledged.

"Trust me," I called. "I can handle anything you've got."

She walked backward, laughing, and said, "We'll see about that."

Yeah, she couldn't ignore a challenge either. I liked that. I liked *her*. I didn't know her name, but that was only one of the things I intended to discover. I watched her go, following the lines of her toned calves and the sway of her hips.

"Who was *that*?" Will asked.

"Don't know," I said. I scratched my jaw as her silhouette faded from sight.

"Really?" Will asked. He set his board on the sand and grabbed a rock from a nearby tide pool. He turned it over in his hands, and then sent it skipping across the surface of the water. "You two looked…familiar."

I jerked a shoulder in response. "Not exactly."

He gazed at me, his hands on his hips and his lips flat. He pointed to my abandoned surfboard a couple yards away. It was on its back and gathering a sizeable quantity of seaweed around the fin. "What's that all about?"

"I hit the waves this morning," I said. "They hit me back. More like whupped me and sent me cryin' to my mama."

He cocked his head to the side, his eyes narrowed, and stared down at me. Apparently determining that I couldn't be left on my own, he dropped beside me. He didn't say anything, and neither did I. We'd both walked away from the Navy with wounds and war stories, but we didn't make a habit of discussing any of it.

"Do you miss the Teams?" I asked eventually. I'd been out of the military since my injury, but Will only had a few years of separation. For most, the Special Teams was a lifestyle, a family in its own right.

Will laughed. "*No*," he said. "And neither do you. Think about it. When was the last time you had blisters inside blisters? Or packed a gunshot wound with dirt? Or pissed in a plastic bag? Or ate freeze-dried food by choice? There's none of that arugula you like in the Navy."

"That's just the bad shit," I said with a scoff. "What about the missions? And the guys?" I rubbed my neck as I thought back. "I miss the guys."

Will snickered. "You miss the adrenaline of the missions. You don't miss getting shot at," he said. "If you need guys, come back to Boston with me. I'll give you some guys. Shannon's brothers could use a trip to SERE school."

"I might wear suits and eat arugula now, but I don't need to hang around with your architect brothers-in-law," I said. "I mean, maybe I would. I don't know. I have guys. I don't need you get me guys."

Will swung his head toward me, his brows

furrowed. "Is that why you're so pumped about expanding the training site? Because you want to get involved in missions and hang out with Team guys?"

"No," I said. "That's not it at all. We're able to take on bigger clients if we're able to offer stronger units, and we need a larger, more flexible facility than the one we're working with to accomplish that. I'm thinking about the bottom line."

"The bottom line was pretty healthy last month," he replied. "And every one of the twenty-two months before that, too."

I drove my hands into the sand and let the grains slide through my fingers. "Staying on top of spycraft is expensive work, Halsted. We can't get complacent."

He grabbed several more rocks and rolled them around his palm. "You're in a private jet co-op, Kaisall. We're past complacency when you're playing with that kind of money."

"Only because it's more efficient with my travel schedule," I replied.

"It's still a *private jet*," Will said. He dug his toes into the sand and stared at the ocean for a minute. "This isn't about money. We're doing just fine, and you know it. You're bored. You need some action in your life. Working and busting my balls cannot be the sum of your existence." He rubbed his palms together and glanced at me. "You need dude friends."

"Why would I need friends when I have you to point out all of my issues?" I asked.

"You gonna see that brunette again? She seemed

very," he started, cupping his hands in front of his chest in the international signal for *that rack, though*, "intelligent. More—ah—*better* intellect than Titsy O'Silicone."

"Yeah, very *intelligent*," I said. I gazed down the beach in the direction she'd gone. All I knew was that she had a friendly smile and stopped for strangers whimpering on the shore, and that was reason enough to see her again. At her apartment. At night. "Don't wait up for me, sweetheart."

"Now that's an action plan," Will said, clapping me on the back. "That's the kind of excitement you need. Don't forget the protection."

"Do you trust me *at all*?" I rolled my eyes. "I don't go anywhere without a sidearm. You know that, Halsted."

"I meant condoms," he said, dropping his head into his hands with a laugh. "Condoms, Kaisall."

"Oh, yeah," I said, shrugging as if rubbers were on the top of my mind. They were not.

"May I offer some advice?" he asked.

I scowled at him, my eyes narrowed. "What the fuck has this conversation been if not an accounting of my many faults and your sage solutions?"

He flipped me off. "It's Montauk, dude. Bring the condoms. Lock up the sidearm."

CHAPTER FOUR

I KEPT MYSELF BUSY ALL DAY, AND WENT TO GREAT lengths to keep my eyes from watching the clock. In large part, I succeeded, although I did save an entire hour to travel the two miles from my house to her bakery-top apartment.

That meant I was driving in circles around Montauk for fifty-five minutes, and reading the newest posts from a Special Forces blog that I favored while parked on a side street for another ten because I couldn't show up at the stroke of eight. I might be into this woman—whatever the hell her name was—but I wasn't needy. Fuck no. The last thing I wanted was to be following her around like a lost mutt.

I scrolled through a few more blog posts—one about a new rifle with some unnecessary features, one about a movie that did a piss-poor job of depicting military life, and one complaining about politicians who'd never served a day in their lives—and by the time I was finished, it was almost eight thirty.

The alley behind the bakery was narrow and dark, and no lights illuminated the rickety staircase leading to the loft apartment. I paused to scowl at the shoddy setup. Nothing annoyed me more than the lack of basic security protocol. This was fucking ridiculous, and for a woman living alone? Really fucking ridiculous.

The only saving grace was that the stairs were too wind-worn to be quiet. Every one of my steps was greeted with the squeal and creak of old wood. It was a miniature, fully inadequate alarm system, and it worked because she appeared at the door before I was halfway up the stairs.

Her hair was tied back in a braid, and a long, loose tank top ghosted over her curves and swirled around her thighs. She was wearing leggings that ended just past her knees, and her feet were bare. She didn't look much different than she did this morning, but it was somehow *more*. More striking, more interesting, more arousing.

"Wasn't sure you'd come," she said, leaning against the open screen door. "Didn't know if you were scared off, or if you'd rise to the occasion."

There were those innuendos again. I'd never met a woman who traded in thinly veiled penis humor before. Or perhaps I hadn't met one who did it this effectively. "Not much scares me, ma'am," I said.

"Did I just catch of hint of the South in that *ma'am*?" she asked.

"Guilty," I said, my hands spread before me. My time away from the Delta had softened my accent. It lived on in certain words and phrases, and came roaring to life whenever I was in the company of true Southerners. Or copious amounts of liquor. "Sometimes I can't help it. It just pops up."

She laughed as I stopped two steps away from her, and it was a raw, unfiltered laugh. I could roll with a chick who appreciated dick entendres. "Sounds like a hard situation."

"If you only knew how hard," I said, and her gaze dropped straight to my crotch. I hadn't experienced levity like this in months, and it was going to my head like champagne on New Year's Eve. It was perfect.

"I could guess," she said, winking. "Come on in, big guy. Let's do some work on those aches and pains of yours."

She ushered me inside, and the aroma of incense —or whatever it was that smelled like dirt, herbs, and old tea all at once—was the first thing to hit me. It should've been awful, but it wasn't. It was heady, and had the back of my neck tingling.

This was followed by the realization that her apartment was no bigger than a postage stamp. Opaque screens forced a bit of division, and added a trace of legitimacy to the sheet-draped massage table that stood just inside the space. The lights were low, and the shadow of a late summer sunset lingered.

Her place was more of an attic than anything else, yet thoroughly lived-in. There was an old-fashioned trunk in the corner, and the lid was covered with dozens of books. A small, slouchy sofa was tucked off to the side, and an afghan hung over its back. There was a wide coffee table, on it a bowl full of zucchini, cucumbers, and tomatoes, and a half-completed puzzle.

I was staring at the refrigerator, and the takeout menus trapped under a chunky magnet in the shape of a lobster with "Montauk" painted on it, when she cleared her throat.

"Okay, now tell me about that leg," she said. "Do you see a physical therapist for regular work? I don't want to trample on any treatment you're already getting."

I turned around and dipped my hands into my pockets. "I want to know your name," I demanded.

She touched her fingertips to her forehead as if realizing right then that we'd skipped that step. "I'm April. April Veach."

I stretched my hand in her direction. "Jordan Kaisall," I said. "Spring baby, huh?"

April's brows furrowed and she cocked her head to the side. "Why do you say that?"

"Why would you be named April if you weren't born in the spring?" I asked. I couldn't understand such a thing. "Unless it's a family name, at which point *someone* was born in April."

She looked irritated for an exceedingly long

moment, and then dropped her hand to my forearm with a laugh. "I had you going there, didn't I?" She squeezed my arm, and I wanted to touch her more than anything right now. I didn't. All humor aside, I hadn't been offered the privilege yet. "I arrived a bit late. May first. After everything I'd put my mother through, she decided she was sticking with April."

"What kind of acupuncturist are you? Busting my balls and making dick jokes?"

April shot me a bright smile but edged away from me.

Come back here. Touch me again.

"The best kind," she said, jerking a shoulder as if it was totally obvious.

"You're snappy," I said. "I like it."

A surprised smile brightened her eyes. "All right, big guy. On the table, on your back. Lose the shirt and shoes." For the second time tonight, she checked out my crotch. My cock wasn't one to stir at every warm breeze and short skirt, but this type of attention was something else altogether. "The shorts can stay unless they get in my way."

They're getting in my way.

April watched as I yanked my shirt over my head, sucking in a breath when my skin came into sight. She studied my chest, her eyes mapping each dip and ripple, before turning on her heel and busying herself at a small cupboard near the table.

"I know it's still really warm," she started, "but I was thinking we'd begin with hot stones to address some of the secondary strain you're experiencing in your hips and shoulders. Would that be okay, or do you think it would be too much heat for you?"

She pivoted as she tied a small apron around her waist. She stole another look at my abs, but she was frowning while she did it.

"What are you waiting for? Get on the damn table like you were told," she said.

"Yes, ma'am," I replied, gingerly hoisting myself onto the surface. I wasn't convinced this thing would hold my weight. As it was, my feet were dangling off the end, and my shoulders were extended over the sides.

"Mmm, you really are a big guy," she murmured, noticing my awkward position.

"You have no idea, honey." It was spoken under my breath, but April heard every word. That earned me an arched eyebrow and swatted shoulder, and it was entirely worth it.

"Now, tell me how you feel about heat. Is it too warm for hot stones? I don't want you pickling in your own sweat," she said.

"I can take as much heat as you have to give, ma'am," I said, smiling up at her.

And I'd really like some give and take with you.

"Yeah, I'd like to see you try," she murmured, a laugh lingering in her voice. Her expression sobered and she rubbed her palms together. "Here's what I'm thinking. We'll start with some deep tissue work, and we'll see what we can accomplish that way. I know you're a tough guy, but you have to speak up if anything is uncomfortable. We wouldn't want to make things worse."

"No, ma'am," I replied. I liked her all-business look just about as much as I liked her punny jokes.

I bet you're bossy in bed, too. Let's see how long I let you get away with that.

"Good, okay." She moved to the head of the table and set her palms on my breastbone. "Breathe in…and out," she said, pressing down.

April's hands smoothed over my chest and down my arms, and my body couldn't decide how to react. Her ministrations were both calming and arousing, and I wanted to keep both sensations close.

"How long have you been doing this, April?" I asked.

She hummed to herself as she slipped smooth— and really fucking hot—stones under my shoulder blades. "Massage for about six, um, seven years," she said. "Reiki and acupuncture are more recent studies, both in the past few years."

She moved more stones into place, and then did something amazing with her thumbs on my shoulder that had me releasing a soft moan. Stars danced behind my eyes. "Uh, that is *incredible*," I said.

Don't stop, honey. Don't stop.

April laughed as she moved to the other side. "Just remember that when you're sore tomorrow," she said.

You can leave me sore anytime you'd like.

"Looking forward to it," I said.

She dropped a hand to my sternum and leaned over to catch my eye. "You know, most people lie there, close their eyes, and enjoy the treatment," she said. "You can't just take it, can you?"

"I can take it," I said, grabbing the tail of her braid between my fingers when it slipped over her shoulder. She lifted an eyebrow but didn't comment, and I continued toying with her hair. It was silky, almost like satin. I thought about dragging those strands over my lips, feeling her softness and inhaling her scent.

April walked her thumbs up the back of my neck and I groaned at her touch. "How's the pressure?" she asked.

I will die right now if you stop.

She wasn't aiming for innuendo of any sort, not with the quiet, professional tone, but that was the only thing my ears heard. I tugged her braid, drawing her attention back to my eyes. "Harder," I said, grinning at the amusement in her smile. "I want it harder."

"That's what they all say," she murmured.

"Is that how you like it?" I asked. "Harder?"

April offered a quick smirk that was either intended to shut me up or confirm my suspicions, but she didn't respond. With the aid of another hot rock, she rubbed my shoulders into a state of brutal bliss. The ability to form complete thoughts soon drifted away, and I sank into the serenity her touch offered.

Eventually she turned her attention to my leg, and seeing her study the silvery lines that covered my skin pulled the tension back into my neck. I gestured toward her, and said, "Don't worry about it. A lot of people have tried to help, and there's nothing—"

April held up a hand to silence me. She was good at that, shutting me up and shutting me down. "No, no. No arguing from you. I'll do what I do, and you can tell me if it helped when I'm finished," she said.

She dropped her palm to my thigh and squeezed. It was probably meant to be reassuring or soothing, but it only had my dick leaping for her attention. "You're the boss here," I said, holding my hands out in surrender.

"I need to know more about your injury," she said. "You mentioned it was about fourteen years old, and I'm guessing there are plates and screws in there, right?"

"Total knee replacement," I added.

She hummed as she continued examining my leg. "But you're still having considerable pain," she said, mostly to herself. "We're going to work on that, okay? I might not be able to eliminate all of your discomfort, but I can put a dent in it."

"Sounds like a good plan," I replied.

Just don't take your hands off me.

Instead of rocks, April produced some chilled cloths and layered them over my leg after she worked each area. She was gentle now, but never tentative. She wasn't afraid she'd hurt me like all the other practitioners I'd visited in the past, and that confidence was encouraging. It helped me get through the uncomfortable moments, and granted my mind tons of room to imagine her fingertips sliding under my shorts.

It was the kind of idea that required little air to take flight. I saw her straddling me on the table. Bent over the table. Up against the refrigerator. In bed, slow and sweet. There were no limits to what I wanted with her.

Aside from the small issues of whether she wanted any of it too, and not knowing her at all.

"Is this your primary gig? Massage and acupuncture?" I asked. "Or is this the side gig?"

"I have a bunch of gigs." April kept her gaze on my leg but shook her head. "I do a little of everything," she said. "I work on wedding cakes, teach yoga, do bodywork. I like variety. Spice of life, you know?"

Touch me there, everywhere. Please.

"For sure. Baking wedding cakes sounds like a good time," I mused. "How do you get into something like that? Culinary school?"

She unscrewed the lid on a small mason jar and retrieved a honey-like substance from inside. "Hold that thought. This is a certified organic medicinal cannabis balm. A couple in Rhode Island makes it by hand, and it does wonders for deep muscle, joint, and ligament pain," she said. "It's not marijuana and it won't get you high, but given the way it's compounded, a tiny, *tiny* amount of THC could show up in a drug screening. Some people avoid it because they don't want to run into problems at work."

I snorted out a laugh. "That won't be an issue where I work," I said. "I'm the CEO."

"What I'm hearing is that you're good with the balm. Got it." She rubbed it in her palms before bringing it to my knee. "To answer your question, I don't bake the cakes. I just decorate them. I sculpt the edible flowers and lace and stuff like that. Sometimes I paint cakes, but most people want the fondant designs."

"Only wedding cakes?" I asked. "Or are you open to other occasions?"

With the balm worked into my skin, April wiped her hands on one of the discarded cloths before moving to my waist. She squeezed my hips, nodding to herself, and shoved several more hot stones under my back.

"I'm open to all occasions," she said. "But it's the wedding season that keeps me busiest."

"What do you do when it's over?" I asked. "I don't think there are too many winter weddings in Montauk, but I could be wrong about that. I'm not up-to-date with my *InStyle Weddings* reading."

"That's funny," she murmured. "Neither am I."

I was partially curious about this and partially building up my base of knowledge before angling her into bed. I didn't have anonymous, random sex with women now or anytime previously, and I wasn't about to start. Sure, I liked casual relationships, and sex didn't have to be complicated, but it didn't have to be empty either. I believed in liking a woman's personality as much—if not more—than her pussy.

Obviously, my judgment of Jocelyn had been flawed. Everyone deserved at least one mulligan, right?

"You're right about wedding season," she said, squirting oil into her palm. "Montauk gets pretty quiet once the summer ends, but it's all good. That's when I work on gingerbread villages." She pointed at my crotch—I was starting to crave this unabashed attention—and then met my eyes. "Can you push them down a bit? I don't want to get oil on your clothes but I need access to your lower obliques."

Without breaking eye contact, I unbuckled my belt and kicked my shorts off, leaving me in a pair of low-slung black boxers that did nothing to conceal my growing arousal. "How's that?" I asked.

April tucked her bottom lip between her teeth and rocked her head from side to side as she stared at the bulge in my boxers. "Not complaining," she said with a shrug.

"That's good to hear," I said. "I take satisfaction very seriously."

That earned me another indecipherable smirk, and she settled back into her professional mode. She moved the stones around, swapping them out for warmer ones that she had stowed somewhere beyond my view. It was amazing that she could accomplish so much with her slim fingers and some rocks.

"What was that about gingerbread houses?" I asked, suddenly recalling our conversation.

"Mmhmm." She nodded as she drove her knuckle into my waist. "Around the holidays, some hotels and restaurants feature gingerbread house displays. There's a resort in Arizona that has a gingerbread railroad and town in the lobby every Christmas. I worked on that once. There's a furniture shop outside Boston that commissions a huge gingerbread model of their first storefront from decades ago. I usually head up there for a month or two in the fall, to get it ready for the holiday rush. They're fun projects. Easter egg installations used to be popular. Four-, five-foot-tall eggs sculpted from cake and decorated. Not much demand for those recently."

"That's interesting," I said. "And a little random."

"I like random," she said, shooting me a cheeky smile. "I like having a range of unique skills that I can take anywhere in the world."

April's work on my shoulders and leg was incredible, but something about her hands on my waist and hips was completely different. The proximity to my needy, single-minded cock meant that every touch was a tease, a promise of more to come. And those promises gained certainty as her fingers swept just beneath the band of my boxers. It was light and quick, but I didn't know how much longer I could keep my hands to myself.

Of course, I was *capable* of keeping my hands to myself. It was that I didn't want to, and after that near dick-grazing experience, I wasn't convinced she wanted it, either.

"Do you travel much?" I asked, a throb of need catching in my voice.

"Some," she replied. "I love the American Southwest in the spring, New England in the fall. Or Rome in the spring, and London in the fall. Summers in Prague, and winters in Vancouver are my favorites. There's never a bad time to visit Tel Aviv or Haifa."

"That sounds like more than 'some' travel," I said.

"Perhaps." She layered her hands over each other as she worked my hip, and I stole that moment to admire the firm lines of her body. I'd never believed that yoga made for drool-worthy backsides, but I stood corrected. "I'd like to travel more, but I also like spending time in places, getting comfortable."

I reached out and grazed my fingers along the side of her thigh. "Are you comfortable here?"

Tell me you want this. Tell me you need it as much as I do.

April glanced down at my hand and then back up at me. There was a quick tilt of her head followed by a sweet smile. "I'm very comfortable," she said, her words laced with meaning. "Are you?"

I ran my hand up her spine, to the back of her neck. She leaned into me—just barely, only enough that I felt it in her muscles rather than saw it—and that was when I decided I could get to know her *while* taking her to bed. I was nothing if not efficient.

"Is this almost over?" I asked, my hand gliding

down to squeeze her backside. Yoga did this body all kinds of good.

April's hands froze on my hip. "What's wrong? Are you experiencing more pain?"

I pointed to the erection straining against my boxers. "A little bit, yeah," I said.

She shook her head and offered my cock an arched eyebrow, all while suppressing a laugh. "It's not that kind of massage," she said.

I gave her ass another squeeze. "What kind of massage?" I asked, feigning a good deal of outrage. She gave my crotch a pointed look, and *oh God*, I just wanted her hands on me. "You don't think I'm looking for some kind of happy ending, do you?"

Please touch me. Wrap those beautiful fingers around my cock and stroke me. Hard. Rougher than you think I'd want.

"I find that insinuation appalling," I continued. "Happy endings—*I'm told*—are the sexual equivalent of an oil change. Basic. Perfunctory. Soulless. Not to mention one-sided. Really, April. Don't you believe I'm better than that?"

Her shoulders shook with silent laughter as she drew her focus toward my flank. "You're carrying a lot of tension," she said. "Here. Your shoulders. Your hips. Probably along your spine, too. Why don't you turn over and let me work on your back?"

I loosened my hold on her backside, and dragged my knuckles over her upper leg. "Your hands have been all over my body. To my mind, I'm long overdue in returning the favor," I said.

A breath whooshed out of her. She tipped her chin, staring at the ceiling with her hands propped on her hips. It made me reconsider continuing to caress her thigh, but then I remembered how she softened when I gripped her neck. She would've slapped my hand away if my touch were unwelcome, or clocked me with one of those rocks.

When her gaze returned to me, the smirk was gone. April eventually said, "I've not seen you around town. Are you vacationing? Visiting for the weekend?"

If she was wearing underwear, it was a thong. My fingers had yet to find evidence of a single panty line, but I was one relentless motherfucker. I was committed to this endeavor now, and I continued mapping her curves. "I'm here for the weekend, yeah," I said. "I have a place on Ditch Plains but I don't make it down to Montauk as often as I'd like."

"Since we only have this one weekend..." April smiled, half shy, half smirk. "We should—"

I didn't wait for her to finish, instead arching up and driving my fingers into her hair. I hauled her against me, stealing her lips. I'd expected her to be sweet, like buttercream or gingerbread, but she tasted of something stronger, richer, like a rare variety of honey. And *oh*, she felt like heaven against my mouth.

"Thought you'd never ask," she replied.

"Bed," I said against her lips. "*Now*."

I pushed away from the surface, careful not to topple the table and send us both tumbling, and hooked my arm under her ass. It was fucking fantastic having something worth holding onto there.

"Mmm," she purred against my jaw. "You shouldn't be lifting me. I'm too heavy, and I just spent the better part of an hour working the knots from your quad. I don't want you straining yourself."

I tilted my head back as I shuffled around the room-dividing screens and inconveniently placed furniture, wanting to catch her espresso eyes before responding. She was busy dragging her palm over my chest and leaving a trail of hungry kisses on my neck, and didn't notice me watching.

"Your time for worrying about my leg is over," I murmured, squeezing her ass for emphasis. "Listen here, beautiful. You've been running this show and doing a damn fine job at it, but it's my turn now. Are we clear on that?"

A laugh burst from her lips, and that response sent my eyebrows arching up. Her only clarification came in the form of her teeth scraping over my earlobe, and there was no way for me to interpret that as dissent. It only took a few steps to reach the bed, and I was yanking off her leggings the second her back hit the quilt.

"You won't be needing these," I said, peeling the dark fabric from her legs. My eyes widened when I spotted a wisp of pale lace nestled between the globes of her ass. I hooked a finger around the thin band circling her hips and pulled it away, then let it snap back. "I've been debating whether you were wearing a thong or nothing at all."

April stared at the bulge in my boxers before meeting my eyes, and a slight smile was curling up the corners of her lips. "You must've been debating it really hard," she said. "I'd like to get my hands around it, but it looks like a thick topic."

Growling, I fisted the thong and tore it from her body. The tattered fabric was feather-light in my hand, but it was the stone holding the dam together. I stared at the lace while every nerve and muscle in my body aligned for the singular task of devouring this woman.

And that was what I did. The bed creaked when I dived between her legs, sucking and licking and losing myself like I hadn't tasted a pussy in years.

Then again, I'd never tasted pussy as good as hers, and that was why I was eating her like she was my last meal.

"Jordan," April purred. She raked her fingers through my hair, rubbing and pressing my scalp as she went. "*Jordan*. Slow down. This is going to be over too quick."

I shook my head and hummed in disagreement against her clit. I wanted to memorize her sounds, the feel of her against my tongue, the way her body tightened when I pumped two fingers inside her. How she came for me hard and unbelievably fast.

"How was that, honey?" I asked, dragging my gaze up the length of her torso.

"I think you know," she said, a breathless laugh thick in her voice.

Heat was creeping over her chest and cheeks, and her lips were parted as if she was about to speak—or scream. Her braid was trapped under her shoulder. There was something gorgeously disciplined about that plait, but I wanted her dark hair spread out on the pillows, tangled in my fingers, sliding over my skin. Levering up, I reached for the tail, and loosened the tie.

"Better," I murmured, kneeling between her legs. My cock was drilling its way out of my boxers and my lips were slick with her arousal. I reached for her destroyed thong, discarded on the corner of the bed. I dragged it over my face.

"*Ohmygod*," April panted.

"Off," I said, motioning to her tank top.

"You too," April said. She pointed at my boxers before tugging the shirt over her head. I hooked my thumbs in the fabric but wasn't going any further until April was naked. A bra-type thing was waiting beneath. It was sexy and cute, but I didn't care about that shit right now. I just wanted a face full of tits, and that complicated thing was in my way.

"Off," I repeated, my tone leaving no room for argument.

Her eyes narrowed, and I couldn't determine whether she was about to fire back or follow orders. A moment passed, and this standoff had my cock throbbing for her. Then off it went, and I didn't even blink before drawing her nipple into my mouth.

"The drawer," April panted. "Condoms. In the drawer." She tried pushing my boxers down but failed each time as my dick was snared just beneath the waistband. Sitting up, she curled one hand around my aching length and used the other to vanquish my underwear. "If you don't get a condom right now, Jordan, I'm gonna think you misinterpreted all those comments I made about your cock."

"No, ma'am, I did not misinterpret a word," I said, rolling my hips with her lazy strokes. It was like her body knew how to meet mine, and all I had to do was let myself savor it. "Your hand feels—aw, fuck—keep doing that, honey."

"Check the expiration dates," she said. "On the condoms. I think some of them might be pretty old. I haven't had sex in forever."

Nope, I didn't need to savor. Not when I had a lonely pussy to save.

"No need," I said, going in search of my shorts. "I brought a fresh supply."

Propped up on her elbows, April watched as I produced a foil packet from my pocket. "Either you were exceptionally confident or you're living life to the letter of the Boy Scout law."

I returned to the bed and settled between her legs. "That you're able to carry on a conversation with me right now indicates that my clit-licking game needs work," I said. Once I had the condom rolled down, I gripped my cock and admired the beauty before me. "How about I fix that now?"

————

"STROKE MY EGO A LITTLE," I said. Completely straight-faced, April reached over and pumped my spent cock. It roused under her touch, but after three extremely satisfying rounds that resembled my personal homerun orgasm derby, some recovery time was in order. "How long had it been for you?"

She chuckled, wincing, and said, "A little more than a year and a half."

I gathered her close and kissed her forehead. "You poor thing," I said.

"Save your pity," she said. "It was a self-imposed vow of chastity. One can't be hopping into bed with the locals one night and then delivering their granny's birthday cake or working their sciatic nerve the next morning."

"Does that mean you don't date all the men you find washed up on the beach?" I asked. "The surf can be pretty wicked out there. I can't be the only one eating sand."

"Actually, no," she said with a laugh. "I don't use the waves as a matchmaking service." She nuzzled her head against my chest, and I pulled the sheets up to her shoulders. "Present company excluded."

"It must've been an amusing sight, me wiping

out," I said ruefully. "What's the Montauk equivalent of roadkill? Driftwood? Beached whale?"

"Would you stop it?" she asked, exasperated. "It wasn't that bad, Jordan. The worst part was getting blindsided by your board."

"She saw the whole sordid thing and still took me to bed," I mused.

April edged up on an elbow and met my eyes. "You know what I thought when I first saw you out there?" she asked. I shook my head. "I thought *who is that fuck-hot beast on the longboard*? I had no idea who you were or where you'd come from, but I knew I wanted to do incredibly rude things to you."

Recovery time? I'd forgotten all about that shit.

"The truth comes out," I said, pinning her to the bed. With her legs hooked over my hips and her fingers clawing at my back, I rocked against her, my cock thick and heavy in her heat.

She smiled me, her eyes glittering. "It has a funny way of doing that," she whispered.

CHAPTER FIVE

THE SCENT OF BREWING COFFEE WAFTED OVER ME, and I shook off the last clouds of sleep. I reached across the bed, waiting for the feel of warm woman under my hand, but I only found rumpled linens. That wasn't what—or *who*—I wanted. Still boneless and sated from last night, I was unwilling to open my eyes. I didn't want this to be over. Instead, I pressed my face into the pillows and growled.

The mattress dipped and April's hand coasted over my shoulders. "Always this grouchy in the morning?"

"Only when I expect a naked woman in bed with me and can't find one," I grumbled.

"Some of us have to work," she said. "I have three hundred fondant roses to make this morning, and some in-home Reiki appointments this afternoon."

She was sitting beside me, her legs crossed. Her hair was damp and loose, and the strands were brushing over my bicep. She was dressed, too, and I didn't care for that. I knew it was late, much later than my usual five a.m. wake-up, and I'd probably long overstayed my welcome. I didn't care for that either. I wanted more. More of this, more of her, even more dick jokes.

I curled around her hips and pushed up her shirt to expose the small of her back. "I work," I replied, my lips ghosting over her skin. "I work all the fucking time. I just got back from eleven days of international travel and shoveling one pile of bullshit after another. This is the first time I've taken a few days off since visiting my mother for Christmas. I took her to Disney World."

"Disney World?" April glanced over her shoulder at me, shaking her head like she couldn't imagine me at an amusement park.

"And Universal Studios," I said. "I angled for a trip to the Goldeneye resort in Jamaica, where Ian Fleming wrote the James Bond novels, but she was set on Orlando. She'd never been."

April ran her fingers through my hair. "You're not supposed to be such a good guy."

"I can be good," I said. I reached up, beneath her shirt and bra, and circled her nipple with my thumb. She released a small pant as her skin tightened under my touch. Then I pinched, and was rewarded with a sharp gasp. "I can be bad, too. There's no reason to choose sides."

She murmured in response and dropped her hand to my bare thigh. I was expecting her to stroke my cock and make this morning a little sunnier, but she slapped my ass instead.

"I'm choosing the side of staying employed," she said, disentangling herself from my hold and pushing away from the bed. My shorts and underwear sailed over her shoulder and landed on the pillow beside me. Nothing subtle about that.

Once I was dressed, I worked on making the bed. It was equal parts Navy-born habit and a ploy to steal a few extra minutes in April's company. When I was satisfied that the sheets were tight, the quilt was straight, and my erection wasn't too obvious, I joined her in the small kitchen area.

"I'm taking you out tonight," I said while she poured some cream into her coffee. "Be ready. How does eight sound?"

She offered me a crooked smile and sipped her coffee. "I'm not really an out-to-dinner girl," she said.

"Then what kind of girl are you?" I asked.

Coffee set aside, she pursed her lips as she reached back and started braiding her hair. "I'm the 'walks on the beach, toss all the leftovers into a salad, fall asleep reading' kind of girl."

I spread my hands out in front of me as if our answer was as plain as day. "We'll walk on the beach and eat salads and read until you let me fuck you again, and then we'll fall asleep. Be ready."

She cast her gaze to the floor, her lips folding into a grim line as she continued braiding. I'd said too much. Pushed too hard. Coming on too strong wasn't something I'd ever been accused of, but I'd never met a woman like April before. She was quiet and capable, but also funny and sensual. She didn't want anything from me either. She wasn't grabbing for money or contacts or status. I didn't even know what to do with all that, other than talk to her for hours and claim her body as my home away from home.

"Look, that didn't come out right," I said. "Maybe it came out exactly as it should've, but it made you back away and I don't like that. I want to hang out with you, and my current state of affairs would be greatly improved if you wanted to hang out with me, too. Salads, books, whatever you want."

April pinched her hair with one hand and used the other to wave at my leg. "I want to get some pins in you," she replied. "I think it would help."

I gestured to my torso. "Are you suggesting there were issues with my performance? I'll bend you over that couch right now and show you how much *help* I need."

She rolled her eyes. "And you'd do it without putting any weight on your right leg," she said. "That's why I spent so much time on your left hip and shoulder last night. You need to address the core problem, and treat the ancillary problems you're creating."

I threw my hands up in surrender. "You got it," I conceded. "Give me the full treatment, and then we'll have a salad and read some books. Later, I'll see to your aches."

April resumed braiding her hair, but she couldn't

repress a grin. "I have appointments after I finish up at the bakery, and then I'm teaching a class," she said, twisting a rubber band off her wrist and around her dark strands. "I'll be free around eight again."

I nodded, matching her smile now. Her gaze settled on my bare chest, and her teeth raked over her lower lip.

You can't hide much from me, beautiful.

"What can I bring?" I asked. "If I can't take you out, there's no way in hell I'm showing up empty-handed. My mother would sooner tan my hide than allow such a thing."

She slipped on a pair of athletic shoes and knelt to tie the laces. "She'd whip your six-foot-four, two-hundred-and-fifty-odd-pound hide?"

"She certainly would," I replied, laughing but dead serious.

"Bring some wine," April said after another glance at my chest. She stood and produced my long-abandoned t-shirt from the massage table. She tossed it to me, but I didn't pull it on. "Whatever you like. I'm not picky."

I looked over my shoulder at the stacks of books piled on her trunk. "And what are we reading?"

She drummed her fingertips against her hips. "Don't judge," she warned, wagging a finger at me. "I'm currently on a historical romance kick. You know, dukes, highlanders, viscounts. It's good stuff."

"Right," I said, slightly confused. "Yeah. Sounds

great. I'll just head to the bookstore down the street, and pick up a, uh—"

She held up her hand, cutting me off as she crossed the room. "Have this one," she said, chucking a paperback in my direction.

Charming the Duke, it read. I thumbed through the pages, nodding as I went. I could do this. She laughed as she watched my reactions, and it was obvious that she didn't think I'd go along with this.

"I see that smirk," I said. "That smirk says you don't think I'm going to read this book." I tapped the cover, where a guy who looked like an extra from the cast of *Hamilton* was pawing a chick in a fancy gown. "I'm all over this. I've got a task and purpose, ma'am, and I'm all over it."

April pointed to the watch on her wrist. "Wedding season in the Hamptons waits for no one," she said. "I have a date with ten pounds of fondant."

"And me." The book and my shirt in hand, I stalked toward her until she was backed against the edge of the countertop. "Don't forget about that date with me."

She looked up, her eyes narrowing in challenge. "What do you think you're doing?" she asked.

I nipped at the corner of her mouth. "Getting a taste of you to tide me over until tonight."

"Are you always this"—she arched up, her hands on my shoulders as her lips captured mine for a brief second—"hungry?"

I leaned into her, kissing her with more heat and

meaning than I knew I had to give. "Not until now," I said, my lips hovering over hers.

CHAPTER SIX

"WE MISSED YOU AT DINNER LAST NIGHT."

I glanced up and found Shannon smirking at me from behind a pair of dark sunglasses. Abby's head was tucked into Shannon's shoulder, her chubby fingers tugging on her mother's auburn ponytail. A light breeze ruffled Abby's blonde curls, and she seemed to eye the ocean with interest. She was still working out the mechanics of walking, but swam—extensively supervised—like a dolphin.

"Ma ma ma," she babbled, pointing toward the shore. "Ma ma ma!"

"I know, I know, you want to splash," Shannon said to the baby. "But we have to talk to Uncle Jordan first. We need to hear all about his nocturnal adventures."

Placing my thumb between the pages, I closed the book and nodded toward the ocean, where Will was perched on his board and waiting for the right wave. "I informed your husband that I wouldn't be there."

"He told me," she replied. She inclined her head to peer at the book. "What are you reading? When I saw you out here, I just wanted to know who you were with last night. Now it looks like you've traded in your standard fare of Special Teams memoirs for a bright-eyed and busty virgin. Where have you been and what happened to you, Jordan?"

I gazed at the sand and shrugged. "I met someone."

She pointed to the book. "And she has a required reading list? That's an interesting tactic."

I thought about offering Shannon some casual, half-baked version of the truth where I wasn't counting down the minutes until I could climb those creaky stairs again or contemplating whether I could run my business from Montauk. I wasn't *really* thinking about seeing out the summer here, but the notion was percolating away in a corner of my mind. It was the same corner where I considered going paleo or buying a minor league baseball team, and other bullshit like that.

"No, nothing like that," I said. I held up the book. "We're discussing romantic literature this evening."

Shannon nodded in approval as she set Abby down. She produced an assortment of beach toys for the infant, and then sat beside her on the sand. "I like that author. No damsels in distress or ladies waiting around for their princes."

I eyed the cover as I considered this. I'd been busy managing my reactions to the steamier parts of the story, and hadn't noticed the absence of damsels or ladies. "Right," I said, opening up to where I'd left off. "I liked that, too."

Shannon shot me an arched eyebrow that said she knew I was full of shit. "This is fascinating," she murmured.

I succeeded in reading an entire paragraph before taking the bait. "What's fascinating?" I asked.

Gesturing between me and the paperback with a grin, Shannon said, "You. You're fascinating. You roll with this intimidating, bad ass vibe and you act as though you don't care about much of anything, but then you meet this chick, spend the night with her, and join her book club." She motioned toward me with a tiny shovel. "The whole thing is fascinating."

Stretching my legs out in front of me, I leaned back and watched the waves for a moment. "I can't determine whether you've hidden an insult in there," I finally said.

Abby grabbed a shell and waved it at me, gurgling and cooing in delight. I accepted the gift, and searched for one to give her in return. I figured a smooth rock would suffice.

"Not an insult," Shannon said, laughing. "It's just amusing to see a serial monogamist make sense of a one-night stand. You're mentally reshuffling your calendar so you can spend another long weekend here, aren't you?"

My desire was to dispute this claim, but my phone vibrated with a notification from one of my security specialists that the equipment I'd requested was to be delivered by messenger this afternoon. Behind it was a string of texts from my senior liaisons, all confirming that they'd pick up any meetings I wanted to offload late next week.

In other words...yes. This weekend wasn't close to over and I was already angling for another visit with April. At the very least, planning to address the absence of security measures at her apartment.

"Just because I don't fuck around doesn't mean I'm a serial monogamist," I said. "Maybe if I had some time on my hands, I would play the game a little harder."

"No, you wouldn't." Shannon rubbed my forearm. "I've known you for some time, and I know you're not a player. But there's nothing wrong with being a one-woman kind of guy," she said. "It's a little surprising since most single guys seem to think manwhoring is their job, but it's nice. You don't have a long history of shady behavior to apologize away, and hardly any chance of an awkward encounter with former conquests."

I scowled at her, not entirely pleased with her assessment. I had conquests, dammit.

"Don't give me that face," she said, wagging a finger. "You're a good guy, Jordan. Don't resent that fact. It's a pleasant contrast to your otherwise lethal demeanor."

I chuckled at that, and looked down at my texts. There was one from Mom, imploring me to have fun this weekend. There were six exclamation points, one for every orgasm I put on the scoreboard last night. Not that I was sharing that detail.

She might've helped me launch this business and was one of my most trusted allies, but discussing *intimate relations*—as she preferred to call them—was a hard limit for me. I'd gotten enough of that when I was a kid. My mother had worked the "no sex before marriage" angle hard when I was a teenager. Come to think of it, I could even recall a few lectures as early as fifth grade. She'd never come out and announced that I wasn't to become a teen parent like her, but the subtext was damn clear. There were lectures about diseases and contraception and the remarkable power of sperm to survive for days—*days!*—as it searched for an egg to fertilize.

Abby thrust another shell at me, carrying on in her animated baby talk and forcing me to engage. "Oh really?" I asked, taking the shell. She reached for the arm of my chair and pulled herself up on wobbly legs. "That is amazing. Tell me more."

"Look at you," Shannon murmured. "Nice guy. Good with babies. It's almost like you're not intimidating as fuck."

I swung a glance at Shannon over the baby's head, giving her my best *don't test me or I'll stab you in the throat* face. I didn't mean any of it, and she knew that. My partner's wife was one of my favorite people in the world. She wasn't the sister I'd never had; I didn't think sisters routinely ordered others to suck their dicks. She was a prettier, snarkier version of Will, and one who possessed a bit of insight into my inner workings even when they weren't immediately obvious to me.

"I'll be getting my relationship advice from her," I said, settling Abby on my lap. "She'll take it from here, thank you."

Shannon laughed, completely undeterred. "Just tell me this: are you thinking about extending your stay, or coming back next weekend?"

"I have to be in Texas in a few days," I said. It was meant to call a timeout on this conversation. Unfortunately for my penis and overall happiness, I couldn't stay past Tuesday, not with the mushroom cloud of issues on my desk. It didn't matter whether I wanted to spend every weekend or every minute in Montauk. I wasn't going to get what I wanted, regardless of my serial monogamist status.

Abby yanked off my sunglasses, howling with laughter as she did it. Yeah, a cherub-faced infant besting me summed it all up.

CHAPTER SEVEN

IT HAD BEEN AGES SINCE I'D INSTALLED ANYTHING. I still knew enough of my way around tools and circuit boards to get the job done, but I wasn't quick. It was a good thing I'd arrived at April's apartment a solid three hours before she was due home and expecting me. In that time, I placed several solar-powered security lights and two closed-circuit video cameras that would feed directly to an app my R&D department had designed. April would be able to get a look at anyone in the alley and at her door without stepping outside.

"This is unexpected," she announced from a couple steps below me. There was a tote bag slung over her shoulder and a grocery bag in one hand, and she was fighting a grin. "You brought tools. To my apartment."

I pointed to the alley. "I'm addressing the bullshit situation here," I said. "By itself, the lack of lighting is a serious issue, but you need better security overall. Some closed-circuit video is the least I can do."

She looked around, noticing the lights and solar panels, her head bobbing as she regarded each item. "Yeah, this is unexpected and really quite unusual," she said. "I'm not sure what to say."

"You don't have to say anything." I tapped the video pod above the doorframe. "Consider it my way of repaying you for last night," I said, and then rapidly thought better of it. "The work you did on my leg. The massage. Not the other part."

"Good clarification," she said, laughing. "Finish up this project, and then we can try some pressure points."

I ran my palm over the days-old scruff on my jaw. I wasn't getting away without an acupuncture treatment from April, and I was only hoping that I didn't crumble like a cookie when she started with the stabbing.

"Or we can open some wine first," I offered. "I'd like to talk about that book, too. It was an interesting read. I have some thoughts I'd like to share with you."

"Maybe." April stepped around me and made a show of opening the door to her apartment. "Since we're talking about the state of security here, I think it's worth noting that I don't lock my doors." An impatient rasp rattled in my throat, and she pointed at me. "There's a vein in your forehead that looks like it's about to rupture. You should take some cleansing breaths."

She marched inside, and I couldn't help but collect the things I'd brought with me and follow.

"Why?" I asked. "Why wouldn't you lock your doors?"

April was busy unpacking her groceries, and pivoted to face me. "It's very safe here," she said, gesturing in the direction of the village. "Plenty of people keep their doors unlocked in Montauk."

"You're not one of them," I said through gritted teeth.

She waved a wedge of cheese at me and said, "What? Don't think I can handle myself?"

I set the power drill down and rubbed my forehead. I needed a minute before I could form words other than *Do as I fucking tell you, honey.*

"Just because I like my zen and my namaste doesn't mean I can't kick some ass," she continued. "Honestly, Jordan, the worst thing I'll encounter in that alley is a raccoon. Maybe a skunk."

"Well, now you'll be able to see them coming," I said wryly.

"Even better," she said as she filed her goods in the refrigerator. "This would be a sensational time for you to take off your shirt—"

"You don't have to ask me twice," I said under my breath.

"—and get on the table," April continued.

She pointed behind me, at the massage table, and the joy of getting naked with a gorgeous woman cooled. I scowled at it, even though that was a petty, juvenile response.

While I was fully aware that they were what brought us together, I didn't want this evening to be about my weaknesses. It was enough that April knew of my injuries and daily discomfort. Our entire relationship—or whatever this was—didn't have to center around me and my problems.

April's arms came around my waist, her hands flat on my abs and her head on my back. "You'll enjoy the wine more after I work on your leg," she said, stroking my belly. "I promise."

"This would be more interesting if you were naked," I said. "It would definitely take my mind off the pins you're going to stick into my eyeballs."

She patted my abs. "I'm not going anywhere near your eyeballs," she said with a laugh. "I'm prioritizing your leg, as well as your shoulders. I doubt you'll even feel those. And, if it isn't too much for you, a few spots on your forehead."

I stroked my hand up her thigh. She was soft but solid, and I couldn't wait to get between those legs again. "You won't be naked?" She shook her head against my back. "That's unfortunate."

"It actually matters to me that I treat your leg and ancillary issues. I can help you, and I want you to let me," she said. "On the table."

Chastened, I complied. I couldn't deny that last evening's massage had lightened the discomfort in my leg, or that I appreciated her concern. But all of this was new to me, and I wasn't adept at handling it with grace.

April appeared by my side, and rested her hands on my forearm. "Here's how this works," she said, her words slower, smoother. "I'm going to look for muscular constrictions and reactive areas, and then stimulate those trigger points with thin, sterile pins. I'll use several needling techniques to deactivate the triggers."

"All right," I said. "Let's do this."

She nodded but didn't respond immediately, instead tapping needles into my shoulders. She moved rapidly, too quick for me to process every individual prick.

"How are you doing?" April asked. I heard her footsteps on the floor as she moved around the table, and sensed her near my knee. "Some of these points will be more sensitive than others."

"Ma'am," I said, holding open my palm. "I've been in active war zones. There's nothing you can do to me that I can't handle."

"Is that your background?" she asked. "The military?"

She pressed a needle into the fleshy part of my inner thigh, and fire licked at my nerves.

"Uh, yeah," I said, struggling through the burn. "The Navy. I'm in private security services now."

"Mmhmm," she murmured, her fingers pushing one pin after another into my skin. "Keep breathing. Let your body heal itself."

"I read the book," I offered, swallowing a snarl as a needle pierced the tender side of my knee.

"I'm not surprised. I get the sense you take duty seriously."

Her gaze pinged to the scars on my leg. That she understood it to be a war injury, and one that required no additional explanation, was the saving grace of this treatment regimen. Even after all these years, the details of that mission were still classified above top secret.

"I've been wondering about this all day, Jordan," she continued. "What did you think of *Charming the Duke*? Don't break my heart if you hated it. That series is one of my all-time favorites."

"I didn't hate it," I confessed. "It was a departure from my usual diet of financial reports and newspapers, but I didn't hate it." Another needle near my eyebrow, and it wasn't an uncomfortable sensation, but not an ordinary one, either. "Why do you enjoy it so much?"

"I'm all done," April said. She flattened her hand on my belly. "They'll stay in place for about twelve minutes. You might feel heaviness, perhaps some numbness or tingling. Tell me if you notice that."

"Yes, ma'am," I said. "Why is it one of your favorite books?"

"I loved that Helena was independent," April replied. She took my hand, and started massaging my palm and fingers. "She'd taken charge of her life, and she wasn't troubling herself with any of society's expectations for a woman of her station. And when the bad-tempered duke showed up at her castle, she went ahead and kicked his ass for trespassing."

"But the duke was blind," I argued. "Rafe didn't know he was trespassing. He didn't deserve the beat down that Helena gave him. It was that fuckwit solicitor of his, Mallory, who screwed him over."

"Yeah, Mallory was a douche," April said, rounding the table to work on my other hand. I was started to feel loose, and somewhat disconnected from my body. It was a sensation similar to that of pushing too hard at the gym, and walking out on wobbling legs. "However, you must agree that Helena was extremely generous to let him crash at her castle while he sorted out his affairs."

"Generous? No. That girl wanted to get in his pants," I said. Wobbling legs, wobbling arms, wobbling everything. "She was hot for him from the first minute, even when she thought he was a vagrant."

April paused her ministrations and gave me a sharp stare. "It is possible to look at someone and think, *I want a piece of that fine ass*, but then also think, *You're going down, motherfucker*."

"That's pretty much how you scored me," I said. "Except it was the ocean delivering the beat down, and not you."

"If that's how you want to tell the story, you go right ahead," she said.

"April, honey," I mumbled. I was long past loose,

now sliding into thickness. It was like a dream, or sleepwalking. But sleepwalking through mud and sand. "Is this supposed to feel—uh—um—"

"Yes," she replied, squeezing my hand. "It's known as the *Deqi* sensation. Some patients describe it as a thick, sleepy feeling, and others say it's like slipping into a warm bath, or experiencing a rush of emotions or relief. Some report burning or heat. It varies, and some don't experience it at all, but it's normal."

"I had all of these plans," I said, reaching for her and settling my hand on the curve of her waist. *So luscious.* "I was going to fuck you, like, a dozen times tonight. Now I'm worried that I won't be able to stay awake for that, and you deserve someone who can stay awake."

She chuckled as she resumed the hand massage. "We have plenty of time," she said. "Keep breathing, and just let it happen, Jordan."

"Letting it happen is not one of my tactical competencies, ma'am."

We were quiet for several minutes, and then I sensed her leaning over my body. "I'm going to start releasing the pins," she whispered. "It will be quick, and you shouldn't feel a thing."

"I wasn't prepared for the more, uh, romantic scenes," I said after she'd plucked the pins from my forehead. "I kept looking over my shoulder at the beach, thinking someone would walk up and find me reading about Helena's first time."

"And what a first time it was," she murmured. She was near my knee, and I couldn't reach her.

"Is this what women want? The way Rafe was with Helena?"

"Some," she offered. She was working on my shoulders now, and I hooked my arm around her waist. "But women aren't a monolith. One woman might want to be bossed around and manhandled. Another might want to be the one doing the manhandling."

"And which do you want?" I asked. "I've been wondering about this all day, you know. Whether you gave me this book as an instructional manual. Whether you wanted me tearing your clothes off and taking you up against the wall, like Rafe did in the barn. Or spreading you out and worshipping every inch of your body until you were desperate and begging, like the night Rafe found Helena in his bedchamber." I traced the line of her clavicle and followed it up to her neck, over her lips. "What do you want, April?"

Her throat was bobbing under my fingers, and she swallowed hard. "We're all finished," she said. "How are you feeling?"

I smiled up at her. "I'm good," I admitted. "A little tired, but good. I'd like to hear more of your thoughts on all the ways the duke took Helena."

Her eyebrows lifted as she grinned. "Let me take you to bed."

"No sweeter words have I heard," I said, accepting her assistance as I sat up.

April took my hand and led me to her bed, the one that wasn't big enough and creaked incessantly and was my new favorite hideout. I leaned back against the pillows, and gestured for her to join me.

"What about the time in the library?" I asked. "When he was on the chaise, and she was on his lap?"

"I liked that part," she admitted, curling up beside me. "Helena was in charge and she was taking what she needed from him, but that didn't minimize any of his dominance or strength. I think she finally realized that she was allowed to have needs, and there was nothing wrong with wanting them met." She tilted her head to the side as if seeing the novel—or our thinly disguised talk of desires—from a new perspective. "And there was nothing wrong with wanting Rafe to be the one meeting those needs."

I studied the line of her jaw and cheeks while she spoke, and then touched my thumb to her bottom lip because I adored the plump feel against my skin. "That's what you want?" I asked. "To acknowledge your needs?"

April shook her head and pushed up, straddling my lap. "I don't need any help identifying my needs," she said, her voice laced with humor. "But I'd like to try out that library scene with you."

CHAPTER EIGHT

I REACHED INTO THE REFRIGERATOR AND COLLECTED everything that looked good. All of it.

"What are you looking for?"

After a bit of exceptional Regency-era role-playing and a well-earned nap, we'd shared a meal of wine, crusty bread, and *everything goes in the bowl and somehow it makes sense* salad. It had been great, but my body interpreted lettuce as the precursor to real food.

"I'm making…" I stared at a bouquet of fresh herbs arranged in a mason jar, carton of eggs, and wedge of wax-paper-wrapped cheese. "Scrambled eggs? Do you like that?"

The curtains fluttered as a late night breeze moved through the windows. April leaned back against the headboard, the bed sheets tucked under her arms. Her hair was loose around her shoulders, and a light flush pinked her cheeks.

"Umm," she started, "I didn't process anything you just said because you're naked in my kitchen."

I looked down at myself and shrugged. "You want me to put something on?" I asked.

"No, no," she said, waving away my question. "You make those eggs. I'll just be over here. Watching. I've never had a naked guy in my kitchen before. This is a moment I'd like to appreciate."

"You never answered my question."

"Mmhmm," she murmured as she studied me. My cock was growing heavy under her gaze. "Which question was that?"

Laughing, I reached atop the refrigerator for the cast iron skillet. "Do you like scrambled eggs?"

April continued watching me, her eyes shining with a glimmer of unabashed appreciation that had me questioning whether I needed eggs when I could have her. And she was all that I wanted. It was irrelevant whether it had been two days or two years. There was a weight in my chest, a gravity associated with finding someone who brought levity to my spirit and fire to my soul. It was all in there, gathering volume and intensity, and I didn't know how I'd lived thirty-nine years without experiencing this.

Maybe that was part of the weight. The realization that all of these years had passed, and I'd never tasted an inkling of *this*. I'd dated women for months and even years without wanting to upend my life for them, wanting to promise them everything, wanting so much more with them. The realization that certain things *were* black and white.

"April, honey," I said, my voice thick. "Is that what you want?"

Her gaze moved up my torso to meet my eyes, and a smirk was playing on her lips when she got there. "I love scrambled eggs," she said, and it was as though she knew we were talking about more than a midnight snack. "If that's what you want."

I didn't need to name it or examine it. I just had to let it happen.

"Okay," I said, nodding. We stared at each other for a moment, smiling over this unspoken agreement. "Are you good with cheesy eggs? My mom makes the best cheesy eggs. I don't cook too much, but this is the one thing I can pull off."

April rested her head on her knees when I started cracking eggs into a bowl. "Now that's the third or fourth time you've mentioned your mother," she said. "I take it you're close."

I grabbed a fork from the drawer and whisked milk into the eggs. "She was seventeen when I was born, and she raised me by herself," I said. "We grew up together."

"Does she live around here?"

"No," I said, distracted. Gauging at the stovetop's proximity to my crotch, I decided nude cooking wasn't the wisest idea I'd ever had. I mean, there were risks and then there were grease burns on your penis. I collected an apron from beside the abandoned massage table and pulled it over my head. Once the jewels were relatively safe, I heated butter in the pan. The eggs were quick to follow. "She lives in Mississippi. Near Gulfport."

"Is that where you're from?" she asked.

"Mississippi, yeah." I dug through the drawers and cupboards for a grater, and took the cheese to it once found. "The northwestern part," I added. "The Delta is a lot different than the Gulf Coast, though." I looked back at April once I'd added enough cheese. "Where are you from?"

She rolled her head from side to side before answering. "A little bit of everywhere," she said. "My sister lives near Chicago, and even though I didn't grow up there, I consider it home. I know I can always go there. No matter what happens, I can pack up and spend as much time as I need with Tali. I've sorted out my life and started over in her guest bedroom more than once." She brushed her hair behind her ears and smiled back at me. "Any siblings?"

I angled the pan to chase the remaining liquid toward the heat. "Nope, it's just me," I said. "But there are some guys from my unit who are like brothers. Everyone says it, that the military is another branch of your family tree, but it's true."

"Yeah," she murmured. "I've heard that."

"I'd give my buddy Gus a kidney if he asked," I said, laughing. "I wouldn't care how much he sold it for either." I pulled a plate from the cupboard and spooned the eggs onto it. "Then there's Will. He's a pain in my fucking ass, but I keep him around in spite of it."

"Men are amazing," she said. "If I suggested that my best friends were organ dealers or pains in my ass, people would call me a catty bitch."

"Do it anyway," I said. I settled beside April on the bed and handed her a fork. "Don't worry about that shit."

"Get rid of the apron," she ordered, jerking her chin in my direction.

Smiling, I loosened the ties and chucked the fabric over my shoulder. "How's this?" I asked.

"Haven't decided yet," April said, leaning against my arm. I held the plate between us, and gestured for her to eat. "I'm going to need some more time to look over the goods before forming a conclusion."

She winked as she dug into the eggs, and the weight in my chest expanded like a breath held too long. It wasn't so much uncomfortable as it was an awareness that I needed something I'd been denying myself.

"You can have all the time you want, April."

"That's good news because I'm also going to need you to make these eggs again," she said.

I pressed a kiss to her temple. "Just say the word, honey. I'm yours."

CHAPTER NINE

BALANCING TWO STRING-TIED BAKERY BOXES AND A
tray of iced coffees in one hand, I made my way into
Will and Shannon's house and called out, "Halsteds! I
brought breakfast."

Following the noise, I headed toward the kitchen.
Shannon was rinsing a bowl of blueberries while
Abby drummed her spoon against the tray attached to
her seat. I knew nothing about kids. *Nothing.* But this
one was pretty damn cute.

"Did you say something about breakfast?"
Shannon asked, eyeing the boxes.

"Muffins, croissants, sticky buns," I said, pulling
open the lids to reveal the pastries. "I don't remember
what those two were called, but they look good."

Shannon set the blueberries in front of Abby.
"*Looking good* is a fine criteria," she said. "Sit down,
Jordan. I'll get some plates, and we'll have a tasting
menu. You know, my sister-in-law would love this."

"Goddammit, Shannon," Will said from the patio door. "He can get his own plates. I told *you* to sit down."

"I'm barely pregnant," she replied. "You have another three or four months before you're allowed to go all commando on me."

"There is no *barely* pregnant. You're fully pregnant, and you need to get off your feet." He watched while she collected plates and utensils, and set them on the table. "Indulge me, peanut," he said, gesturing to the whitewashed chairs. "Sit. Eat."

"Only because I want a croissant," she murmured, plucking the pastries from the boxes and arranging them on plates. She glanced at me. "Are these from Seaside?"

"They are," I replied. I reached for a blueberry muffin and tore the top off. That was the best part.

"And what led us to an early morning bakery run?" Shannon asked. She was wearing a bright, knowing grin as she cut the cinnamon knots into even quarters. "Or are we just coming home now? Did the book club run late?"

I shoved half the muffin top in my mouth and offered a small piece to Abby. She pounded it under her spoon.

"This is Kaisall's version of evasion," Will called from behind the refrigerator door. He filled a small cup with milk and set it on Abby's tray. She smiled up at him, and crammed some blueberries into her mouth in a strange expression of gratitude. "It's one of the many reasons we don't let him do any of the actual spy work."

"Fuck you," I mouthed to my partner. I swung my gaze to Shannon. "I stopped by the bakery after leaving April's apartment."

"She has a name and it's April," Shannon said, her tone full of wonder. "Are there any other details you'd like to share with us? What does she do, where is she from—"

"Why is she giving you the time of day?" Will added.

I flipped him off over Abby's head. "She's a cake decorator. At the bakery. And she's an acupuncturist. She also does massage, and, uh—"

What was that other thing?

"Only you would rebound to a Hamptons hipster from a pharmaceutical industry lobbyist, Kaisall," Will said, and at the same moment, Shannon said, "A cake decorating acupuncturist? That's a new one for me."

"She is not a rebound," I argued.

My tone was sharp, as was the glare I shot my business partner. We gave each other a lot of shit and busted a lot of balls. It was in our nature, maybe even our DNA, but I wasn't open to any ball-busting where it involved April. Not yet.

He held up his hands, surrendering.

"She sounds delightful," Shannon said.

"So," Will started, "you're seeing her again?"

I took another bite of the muffin and pried the

beverages from the cardboard carrying tray while I chewed. Cold, strong coffee chased the pastry as I formulated my response. "Yes," I said finally. "While I'm here, yes."

Shannon pointed to one of the remaining iced coffees, and I passed it to her. "Invite her over," she said. "We'd love to meet her."

Will grabbed a chocolate muffin and murmured in agreement. "Yeah, you two should come by tonight," he said. "Unless you already have plans."

I absolutely had plans for tonight, and none of them included a family dinner or Halsted-led interrogation of my—um—what *was* April? I was nearly forty years old and fully opposed to the term *girlfriend* as it applied to April, but it wasn't as though the alternatives were any better.

Lover? No, none of that.

Hookup? What, was I nineteen again? No.

Paramour? I wasn't even sure what that meant.

Significant other? Oh, hell no. That was too contemporary for me.

There weren't many options for appropriate terms that didn't feel juvenile or strange. I knew only that April was a woman I was seeing, and one I hoped to continue seeing. In particular, I wanted to see her naked from sunset to sunrise.

"Uh, well," I started, but was interrupted by a happy shriek. Abby—thank God for that kid—chose that moment throw a fistful of blueberries at me. It sent her into a fit of infectious belly laughs that kept all of the attention on her.

Once the blueberries were eaten or flung to the far corners of the kitchen, Shannon pushed back from the table and retrieved Abby from her seat.

"We're getting changed," she said to the infant. "And then we're going to the beach. Isn't that right, little lady?"

"I'll be down there in a bit, peanut," Will said to Shannon.

She looked between me and Will, and it was clear that it was now time for the business portion of this breakfast. She nodded, and leaned into him when he wrapped his arm around her shoulders. He whispered something that had her rolling her eyes, and I returned to the remaining pastries on the table.

Will peered at his watch when Shannon was out of the room. "This seems like the right time to talk about Renner," he said.

I shook my head. "Probably not."

"Try again," he said.

With a sigh, I leaned back in my chair, my legs stretched out and my fingers laced over my belly. "I don't have much to tell you," I admitted. "Like I've said, I walked in on Joss and Renner when I got home from Riyadh. I had my apartment swept immediately. Advanced security protocols were initiated. The team found a few bugs."

"A few?"

I rolled my shoulders, stalling. Will and I didn't keep secrets. We didn't have time for that brand of bullshit. But there was something about being infiltrated—and infiltrated with the assistance of my ex-girlfriend—that was humiliating. None of the objective measures of success in this business mattered when a competitor could pull it all out from underneath me.

"Quite a few," I said. "We don't know what, if anything, Renner netted."

Will's brows arched as he absorbed this information. "Is it possible he has something to do with the resignations?" he asked. "I liked those guys. They were good guys. I'm pissed about them leaving."

"Me, too." I shrugged. "But I don't know if Renner was involved with that. It's possible. Most of our turnover comes from guys leaving for another security and military contracting firm, or local law enforcement, but I haven't heard anything around town about him expanding his teams."

"And what about Venezuela?" he asked. "I'm fucking furious about Venezuela. That mission was perfect. Everything was in place, and then it all went to shit. I'm convinced there was something else at play. Another operation, or something." He picked at a cinnamon knot. "If the Agency was down there and didn't give us a heads-up, I will personally burn Langley to the ground."

"Please don't do that," I said. "Our relationship with the CIA is strange at best, and adversarial at worst. Arson wouldn't help matters."

"Fine," he said around the muffin. "But whatever it was, it slipped past all of our intel and surveillance work, and that drives me insane."

"And you think *I'm* not fucking furious?" I asked, slamming my palm on the table. "You don't have to explain this to me. I watched that mission fall apart, and I don't need to have a wife or daughter to understand the stakes."

He grabbed Shannon's abandoned coffee and downed half of it in one gulp. "It's time to play out the worst-case on this situation. Did you take any calls about that operation from home?"

Running my fingers through my hair, I groaned. "Fuck, no. I rarely work at home," I said. "When I do, it's only slide decks for pitch meetings. Not much that could jeopardize a mission there."

"Then where does this leave us?" he asked. "Venezuela was one intel failure and asshole parade after another, then we lost an entire team of operators, and now Renner's got ears in your apartment. None of this is coincidental, Kaisall."

"You think I don't recognize that?" I challenged. "I have all of our best people working on new security protocols and twenty-nine extra layers of encryption on everything, and I know you're analyzing every minute of Venezuela to figure out where it went wrong. What else can we do right now? If we sound the alarms, we'll effectively notify our clients that we can't handle this game."

"Fuck," he murmured. "*Fuck.*"

"My sentiments exactly," I replied. I scrubbed a hand over my face, groaning. "As much as I'd like to put a team on hacking Renner and the rest of the Stillhouse shop, I'm not interested in taking that route yet."

"Why the fuck not?" Will asked. "Aside from the fact you're drowning in new pussy, give me one good reason why not."

Drowning in pussy. I snorted at that. It was a fair approximation of the wake-up call I gave April. "We don't play that way," I said, sobering. "Counterintelligence is one thing. Sabotaging the competition is another."

"You and your fucking ethics," Will muttered. "Why can't you be a cutthroat spy boss who takes out anyone who gets in your way? Really, what kind of shop are we running if you won't put an end to Renner based on the fact he tapped your apartment? His testicles should be in a waffle iron right now."

"My mother would quit," I said, laughing. "She'd hop in that little red Beetle and drive on up to D.C. to spit nails in person."

Will knew that Mom didn't love the lethal nature of our covert operations, or the collateral damage we were willing to accept on certain missions. She was far, *far* removed from the raw details, but she had a good idea what was involved. That was why she preferred booking me on protection consults, like the one I was taking in Texas. She found that work safer for all involved, and somehow less morally bankrupt. It wasn't.

"And we know the entire operation will collapse without Mama Trish," he replied. "But hey—if she came up here, she'd probably chew you out and then feed us. That wouldn't be terrible. I could really go for some of her sweet potato pie."

"You're such an asshole." I snapped my fingers and pointed at him. "Wait. Where's your brother these days? He could get us some off-the-record intel about assets on the ground in Venezuela, and whatever's in the air about Renner."

Will's younger brother Wes was a Navy SEAL turned deep cover CIA operative, and he knew everyone and everything in the international intelligence communities. I hadn't seen him in two or three years, but knew he'd been involved in several complex situations overseas.

"Haven't heard from him in a couple of months," Will said. "He's got his hands full with Russia, but I doubt there are more than fifteen people outside this room who know he's on the Agency's payroll."

"There's no way that could turn problematic," I said, cynicism dripping from every word. I supported dark missions where appropriate, but I was also in favor of tidy exfiltration strategies when it was time to get the fuck out of those missions. Most deep cover agents were left to their own devices.

Will grimaced. "I've told him as much. Not that it did any good," he replied. "You know how he is."

Wes Halsted was to the covert services what Pete "Maverick" Mitchell was to the Navy and *Top Gun*.

He skated on the razor's edge of mortal danger, and did it all with a shit-eating grin.

"My brother aside, we should have enough contacts at the Agency to call in a favor or two without issue. Why not do that?" Will asked.

Because I want to keep this quiet. Because I don't want the entire Beltway knowing I've lost control of my shop.

"Forget I brought it up." I blew out a breath and laced my fingers behind my head. "I'm getting to the bottom of this."

Will regarded me for a moment, his expression hiding none of his disbelief. "And when you arrive at the bottom?"

I didn't respond immediately. It wasn't because I was still working on the end game. No, I knew heads would roll. It was only a matter of which heads and how soon. "I'll get the house in order."

He twisted his wedding band around his finger, nodding. "Keep me in the loop on this, Kaisall," he said, his voice heavy with warning.

"When I have information to share, you'll be the first I call."

Will slapped his thighs and stood. "Let's hit the water. I need to get in a couple of miles. Think you can handle that, or should we grab Abby's water wings?"

"Fuck you," I yelled after him.

CHAPTER TEN

APRIL CROSSED HER ARMS OVER HER CHEST. "ON THE table," she said, her pointed glare sliding between me and the sheet-draped surface.

We were several rounds into this standoff, but I wasn't interested in April the Acupuncturist tonight. I was tense, and I didn't want to explain to her how a sunny Saturday had me wound tighter than the Hulk. Not when I'd left her place light and loose only twelve hours ago.

Will and I'd racked up six miles of ocean swimming, and then I'd dedicated some time to sandcastle construction (and immediate destruction) with Abby. But when the baby went down for a nap, Will and I retreated to my cottage to get some work done. First, we reviewed expenditures for additional encryption and anti-hacking measures. That shit wasn't cheap, and I had a serious thought about sending a bill to Jocelyn.

Then we combed through the data gathered from her devices and the surveillance detail I'd ordered. For her part, she wasn't leading the life of a double agent. No extensive contact with Renner as far as we could tell, no contact with burner phones or dead-end email accounts, no unusual financial activity, no movements that indicated anything beyond ordinary lobbyist life. It was more than likely that she was a pawn in all of this, and that only made me hate Renner more. Joss wasn't perfect and she'd made some shitty decisions in recent days, but no one deserved to be used.

After that, we dug into a new report about the events in Venezuela. We'd been contracted to shut down a human trafficking ring and rescue the hundreds of women and children held captive there, but the mission had gone off the rails. We hadn't succeeded in getting anyone out, and while our team hadn't been compromised in the process, we couldn't risk sending the same one in for another attempt. It would be too easy to tip our hand. That equated to three months of preparation down the drain, and that didn't even account for the people left in extraordinary peril.

So, I was too addled for April's massage table. I didn't want the rocks or the pins or her soft words. I wanted my hands on her body, my mouth on her skin, my cock driving into her. And I wanted her to beg for it.

"On. The. Table," April repeated, her words offering no room for argument.

I stifled a laugh. That assertive tone was real cute, but it wasn't working on me tonight.

"April, honey, it's fine. I'm fine." I held out my hands, reaching for her, but she shook her head.

"Listen to me—"

"No, you listen to me," I interrupted. "You've had a long day, and you don't need to spend another hour tenderizing my leg."

She stabbed a finger in my direction. "Don't do that," she warned. "Don't tell me what kind of day I've had. I'm not a delicate flower."

"I don't know about that," I said, moving closer until her folded arms pressed against my chest. I skimmed my hand down her braid, settling on the small of her back. "I've seen some delicate spots on you. Tasted them, too."

I inched up her tank top and trailed my knuckles over the soft skin at her waist until I reached her belly button.

"Your leg needs some attention," she said, her words faltering as my fingers dipped underneath her leggings.

"Your pussy needs more attention," I said. Her forehead dropped to my chest as I found her clit, and a swift exhale followed. "How about a rain check on the treatment, huh? Let's finish talking about that book and drink some wine and see if I can take care of you tonight."

She shook her head as I took her hand and led her to the living room area, murmuring something I couldn't decipher as we walked. If I knew April—and I was almost arrogant enough to say that I did—I knew she was going to advocate for tending to my aches.

"Treatments are only effective if done consistently," she said when I stopped in front of the slouchy white sofa. "Follow-through is important."

"When was the last time someone looked after you?" I asked, resting my hands on her shoulders. "When are you on the receiving end of the massages?"

"I don't—*ah*." She purred when my fingers kneaded the strength along her spine. "I don't remember."

"It sounds like *you* need some attention," I replied. "Let me give it to you."

We were rooted there, her forehead bowed to my chest and my hands stroking her skin, and nothing about this resembled my life. I didn't give back rubs or make cheesy eggs or spend the night. But here I was, offering up things I hadn't realized I was capable of sharing, and muddling through emotions I couldn't identify.

I dropped down on the sofa and tugged her between my bent legs. "Let's get you out of this," I said, edging her leggings over her hips.

"Jordan, I want—"

I squeezed her hips as I smiled up at her. "Yes. Please tell me what you want."

Instead of waiting for her response, I leaned forward and stamped open-mouthed kisses down her belly and across her hips. She was delicious, and her curves could bring me to my knees.

"Don't stop," she panted. Her hands found my hair, gliding through the strands and fisting as I kissed closer to her center.

"This?" I asked, sliding my tongue through her folds. She was wet and warm there, and her scent was heaven. Her head lolled to the side as her eyes fluttered shut, and she hummed in response. "You have the most perfect pussy in the world."

"Really?" she asked, laughing. Her eyes were still closed. "What makes it so perfect?"

My tongue swept over her clit. I adored that pretty little pearl and the fun we had together. "It's yours," I said honestly.

"*Oh*," she replied, the word a quiet sigh. "Oh."

I urged April closer, and she settled in my lap without hesitation. "You won't be needing this," I said, tugging on her t-shirt. It was loose and off-the-shoulder, and while it was cute as fuck, I wanted it in a pile on the floor. "Or any of the witchcraft you have on underneath."

"Only if you join me," she said, hooking her finger around the neck of my shirt.

I yanked it over my head and pitched it toward the opposite side of the room. "Your move, honey," I said.

All three of her layers—t-shirt, camisole, and bra —followed suit, and I was left groaning at the sight of her skin. My hands latched onto her backside and I jerked her up to her knees. It was the picture of indecency, her center poised over my mouth and her hips undulating with every lash of my tongue.

"Too much, too much, too much," she cried, her nails scoring my shoulders.

I slowed to a lazy circle of the tongue over her clit, gradually building up to more, faster, harder. She required peaks and valleys before finding her release, and learning her terrain was no hardship. Her thighs were shaking as I sucked her clit without relent. "Such a good girl," I rasped.

It wasn't long before April slumped against my chest, her breath fast and her heart hammering. "I need a minute," she panted.

My cock was an iron spike under my belt, and I was feeling selfish, but I wasn't making another move until April was good and ready for me. She'd earned another minute or two to come back down.

"Was that okay?" I asked.

"You're gonna break me," she whispered, her words cracking on a sob.

"Only if you want me to break you," I replied, peppering her forehead and cheeks with light kisses. "I promise I'll always put you back together, honey."

Bobbing her head, April reached for my belt with trembling fingers. "Always?" she asked. "No matter what?"

"Always," I vowed, growling when her fingers curled around my cock.

There was a blur of movement as we pushed my

shorts and boxers to the floor. I sheathed myself, and then April was sinking down on my length.

"I want to break you. I do," I said. "Take you apart and then put you back together as mine."

"Jordan," she said. It was equal parts plea and scolding.

"How do you want it to be, April?" I asked, slamming her down and rocking her body the way I needed it. "You want it like this? Hard, rough? A little dangerous? Can you trust me to do that, and still take care of you?"

I didn't allow her a moment to respond, instead crushing my mouth against hers. My hold on her hips was punishing as I moved harder with each thrust. She fisted my hair, meeting me at every turn. My awareness of everything beyond April and the way her heat held my cock drifted away. This apartment, this town, the entire world outside of our bodies ceased to exist, and with it went my shades of gray. In their place were absolutes, and for once, I was willing to choose a side.

I wanted to love this woman, and I wanted her to let me.

CHAPTER ELEVEN

TIME HAD A FUNNY WAY OF SPEEDING UP EXACTLY when you needed it to slow down. I'd spent hundreds of flights watching the seconds tick by and willing every minute to pass faster than the one before, but it was as if that was a different type of time altogether. It wasn't the same as the moments I had with April. I wanted to slow it all down, and draw it all out until I forgot about everything waiting for me on the other side.

But that wasn't happening. Our time was passing more quickly than I could comprehend, each hot day sliding into another steamy night in April's bed, and the end was approaching. Saturday had faded into Sunday—our first day uninterrupted by work—and it was the most wonderful collection of hours and minutes I'd experienced. I was certain more days like this would be headed my way, perhaps even better ones, but until then I was holding it as the standard by which all others would be measured.

We'd lazed in bed long past sunrise, and that allowed us to miss the morning rush at John's Pancake House. We'd wandered around Montauk Plaza after eating, and stumbled into a bookstore with a respectable romance section. Several titles worthy of our *book club meets try out the sex scenes* endeavor were purchased. Later, we'd walked along the beach, sharing the stray bits of self that emerged when people were really open with each other.

Her loathing of reality television came up when I asked whether she was a *Game of Thrones* fan. I didn't correct her misunderstanding. She was too adorable as she went on about pop culture's dueling obsessions with royalty and semi-scripted competition shows. Instead, I shared my inability to commit to rooting for a single football team. I was a purist, and loved the game but hated the franchises. We agreed that *Step Brothers* was a remarkable film, and Adele's music was too emotional and complicated for us.

She had a love/hate relationship with her sarcasm as it often got her in trouble when people couldn't determine when she was being serious. I begged her to keep every ounce of that snark. I had a love/hate relationship with my scowling and death stares as they got me in trouble when people assumed I meant to murder them. She begged me to keep on glowering.

Neither of us could count a great number of true friends but the ones we had were irreplaceable. I admitted that I felt the need to solve certain—*most*—problems by myself, and never ask for help. I worried that, in thirty years, I'd be the eccentric uncle who took up residence in Shannon and Will's guest room. Or worse—living in a retirement community alongside my mother and her cadre of suitors. April expressed that she loved the freedom and flexibility in her life, but still found herself with the urge to put down roots.

I'd almost offered her some roots in the form of me, any way she preferred. I would've, too, if she hadn't stripped down to her swimsuit and charged into the waves. We'd spent the late afternoon pawing each other under the water and reading on the beach, and that was the makings of my best day.

I felt refreshed and, if it was possible, alive again. I didn't know when I'd transformed into a lifeless drone, but April brought me back. For these brief days, I hadn't been completely weighed down by business issues or the bullshit with Jocelyn and Renner. It was like I'd been marching through the desert in full combat gear, and then April helped me strip some of it off.

We'd tucked ourselves around the wide coffee table in her loft that evening, drinking wine and sparring over the proper way to complete a jigsaw puzzle. The evening had been warm, with the sea breeze offering only mild relief, and she'd asked me who I wanted to be when I grew up.

"Yours," had been the only answer.

Then I'd loved her over and over, letting my body speak promises my tongue couldn't yet form.

It'd been perfect, and everything I'd never known I needed. The thought of this ending brought me physical pain.

For the first time in memory, hustling wasn't my priority. I was due in Texas tomorrow, but I couldn't muster the motivation to prepare for the meeting with Representative Brattis. Not that I couldn't coast through a basic protection services meeting, but I never showed up without doing all of my homework and everyone else's, too. It wasn't my style.

In the back of my mind, I knew I could send one of my protection experts to Corpus Christi in my place. Dashing off some talking points and handing it over didn't sound like the worst plan, especially when that plan would give me another night or two in Montauk.

I would've done it. I would've off-loaded my meetings and duct-taped over the other burning issues, but April required space. That wasn't exactly what she'd said, but that was what I heard while walking her to the bakery this morning. She mentioned that, since I was leaving early tomorrow and she was teaching a late yoga class tonight, it would be best for us to spend the night apart. She made this notion sound reasonable, and maybe it was. My objectivity was long gone when it came to her.

I headed to the kitchen for another beer and then retreated to the back porch. My laptop was around here somewhere, but I didn't want to deal with the Brattis background materials or rehearse the same goddamn security spiel I gave every politician, CEO, and stray billionaire with a sack of dirty laundry.

It was just me, my beer, and the thunderstorm. Despite my best efforts, I couldn't construct a meaningful metaphor with any of it. I sat there, drinking and watching nature's pyrotechnics, waiting for a distraction from the knowledge that April was a stone's throw away and she wanted to be there alone.

Or was she?

The thought wasn't even fully formed before I was cursing myself for being such a jackass. It was possible for a woman to not want my company and also not have another man's balls slapping against her chin in my absence.

"Fuckin' Jocelyn," I muttered.

I closed my eyes and listened to the drum beat of rain and thunder overhead. The rumbling served as a beautiful chorus to the lonely thump of my heart. I was on the verge of falling asleep, the exhaustion of meandering down well-worn paths of bitter loneliness heavy on my shoulders, when I realized the rumble wasn't only coming from the sky.

I made my way through the cottage, beer in hand, and stared at the front door. I figured it was Will. He'd always had a knack for inviting himself in and being annoying. Turning the handle, I asked, "What the fuck do you want, asshole?"

It wasn't Will.

It was April, and she was soaking wet. Clothes, hair, skin, everything. She was small and shivering, and her dark eyes were saucer-wide. I gazed at her, feeling my aggravation drain away and curiosity take its place. Curiosity and a healthy appreciation for the wet t-shirt look, of course.

"I tried," she said. "I tried to make it easy, but I couldn't do it."

I set the beer bottle on the closest surface I could find and beckoned her inside. "Get over here," I said. She came to me, chilled and soggy, and shaking down to the bone.

"I thought it would be better if we had some breathing room," she said as I folded my arms around her. "My life is here, and yours isn't, and we can't change those realities."

"But I'm here now, April, and I have enough resources to change anything," I said, my lips brushing over her ear. "You name it, and I'll make it happen."

"Everything will be different," she said. I was certain I heard her teeth chatter as she spoke.

"We have to get you out of these clothes," I said. I shut the door and towed her toward the small laundry closet near the kitchen. "You could've called me. You didn't have to walk down here in a godforsaken thunderstorm."

She helped me peel the heavy, wet layers from her body and drop them in the dryer. She was left in a damp bra and thong, but her skin was pebbled with goosebumps and her shoulders still trembled. Distressed, I ducked into the bathroom and returned with a towel.

"I wasn't sure I *could* see you," she said, patting her hair with the towel. "I've been walking up and down your street for twenty minutes, arguing with myself."

"Why?" I pulled her close and tucked her head under my chin. "I don't understand what you're saying, honey."

She clawed at me, her hands reaching for my arms, shoulders, anything. "Can I stay here tonight? With you?"

"Of course," I said, still confused. "But first, tell me why you didn't come to the door the minute you got here."

"This is all your fault." Her shoulders were bunched tight and wobbling to work out the chill. "You never warned me that I'd fall for you, and now I have," she said, her chin shaking as a sob broke free. "I can't work my way out of this, and I can't send it away. You're leaving me tomorrow, and I've flat-out fallen for you."

I tugged her into my bedroom and kicked the door shut behind me. "All my fault?" I asked, backing her toward the bed. "Who the fuck are you kidding, honey? You come at me with this luscious body, and the tender heart underneath all that snark, and think *you're* the one falling?" I pointed at the blue quilt and matching pillows. "Allow me to offer a first and final warning: if you get into that bed and open yourself to me, I'm never letting you go. I might leave, April, but I'm never leaving *you*."

She tossed the towel aside and stepped out of my arms, trailing her fingertips over the bed linens as she went. She watched me over her shoulder before drawing the blankets down and slipping beneath them. My shoulders were heaving as my heart slammed against my ribs and my lungs fought to replace the oxygen she'd stolen from me.

"April, honey," I warned.

Her long hair was on my pillows and her bare skin on my sheets, and my cock was pulsing with single-minded desperation. I tore my clothes off and snagged a condom from the bedside table, frantically maneuvering it over my length. She stretched her hand toward me, and I took it, our fingers laced while I joined her under the blankets, claiming my place between her legs. I pushed into her without preamble.

"Never letting you go," I promised, my words spoken directly to her heart as she twined her arms and legs around me.

"Say it again," she whispered.

I did, over and over until the words disintegrated into jagged syllables that made sense only to us.

CHAPTER TWELVE

"I'M MAKING A CAKE REPLICA OF YANKEE STADIUM this morning," April whispered against my lips. "I have to go."

She said this, but she didn't stop stroking my cock over my shorts or edging me closer with a leg around my hip. I might've been the one to back her up against the front door, but it wasn't like she objected.

"I'm not stopping you," I replied. I groaned into her neck when her pace increased, and I was halfway convinced that I needed to mark her there. The other half of me was reminded that I was about twenty years too old for hickeys.

"Use that scary voice," she said, her hips bucking against mine. "The deep one you use to get what you want."

"Scary voice?" I repeated. I yanked her shirt down and sucked her nipple through her bra. "What scary voice?"

April's head thunked against the door as her body arched toward my mouth. "You know which voice," she said, her words breathy. "The one that makes all the panties drop."

"I'm only interested in your panties dropping, honey," I said, moving to her other nipple. "And I'm not scary."

"Bullshit," she said, laughing. "That is bullshit, my friend."

"But I don't scare you," I said. "Do I?"

She fumbled with my belt and zipper, and before I could grumble about her slipping out of my arms, she was on her knees with my cock in her mouth. I braced my forearms on the door as my hips surged forward and a noise that was equal parts growl, groan, and feral cry rattled up from the depths of my chest.

I wanted to hold back a bit. Let her set the pace. I succeeded at that for no more than two minutes before wild, wild need was boiling over inside me. There were no words, just desperate hums and choked gasps, and a steady stream of praise-babble.

"April, honey," I rasped, my hand settling on the nape of her neck. "I'm—I'm—ah, *fuck*."

There was no more cogent thought to be had, but April didn't require further explanation. She nodded, her forehead bumping against my belly, and she squeezed my backside in encouragement. Or what I interpreted as encouragement.

My body was vibrating, every last inch of me, as her tongue worked the underside of my cock. Her short nails bit against my skin, and that slight pinch had my hips snapping in quick, frantic thrusts. There was nothing civilized about this moment, nothing tender. But, *oh, fuck me*, was it amazing.

The roar that heralded my release sounded primal. Dangerous. Maybe there was some truth to April's assertion that I was scary.

I kept a hand on her neck, my thumb rubbing small circles into her skin while she swallowed me down. It seemed endless, as if we'd tapped into a new well of even-better-orgasm stock, and I shuddered as I continued pulsing on her tongue. Heat and sensation buzzed through my body like never before.

I reached behind me, grabbing the collar of my t-shirt, and tugged it over my head. As my cock slipped from her mouth, still full and heavy and ready for more, it painted her skin with the last dregs of my orgasm. Tipping her face up, I wiped her chin with my shirt.

We stayed there, staring at each other, April on her knees and me looming over her. We had to part, her to the bakery and I to the highway, but there were no words. They'd been plucked from the air around us and all that remained was a gaze hot enough to engulf my house in flame.

I'd never experienced a moment like this one—or most of the ones I'd shared with April—but I knew it was the kind where people professed things, promised things.

"You're not getting away from me," I said, running

my thumb over her lips. They were pink and swollen, and I fucking loved it. *Her*. "You understand that, right? Everything I said last night, I meant it. You need to tell me now if any of that's a problem, April, because I'm not letting you get away otherwise."

A breath burst from her lips and she looked away. "Jordan, I—"

The door rattled with a lead-fisted knock. "Kaisall! Get your ass up. The ocean's calling."

My eyes drooped shut and I murmured, "I'm going to fucking kill him."

April gained her feet and stepped away to right her clothing. I let her go but jerked her back to me when everything was in order. With her head on my chest, she asked, "Who are you killing? And why?"

The pounding continued. "Wait a fucking minute," I yelled through the door. "Do you want to meet my business partner?"

Her eyes widened. "I don't want to be rude but I'm really late," she said.

"There will be another time." Nodding, I ran my hand over her silky braid. There would be plenty of time to introduce April to Will and Shannon, and my mother. There was time for all of it. "I'll text you when I get to Texas," I said. "And we'll talk this week."

"Yeah," she said, her shoulder jerking up to punctuate her response. "You know my schedule. Whatever works for you."

I cupped her jaw and brought my lips to hers for a kiss that was meant to be quick and easy, but it turned quick and dirty when I caught a taste of myself on her tongue. I groaned into her, not willing to let go unless we'd succeeded in setting the house on fire.

"Jordan," she panted, her palms flat on my bare chest.

"I know, honey," I said. "I know."

Dropping my forehead to hers to give us a minute to breathe before separating, I drank in the feel of this. I wasn't sure whether this memory would stay true to life over the coming days, but I sure as hell wanted to try.

Will was standing at the end of the driveway when I opened the door, back turned and hands in his pockets. He was intently studying an old tree that had curved with the wind over time, or so it seemed. He played the game well, and pretended not to notice April until she was a few feet away from him. She waved and he nodded, touching the brim of his baseball cap as she passed.

"Good morning," she said.

"Morning," he called. His gaze swung back to me when she reached the road. "And what a fine morning it must be, Kaisall."

"Shut the fuck up," I replied. Turning, I stepped inside but left the door open behind me. "What do you want? Have you finally discovered that you can't knock your wife up any more than she already is?"

"Doesn't hurt to try," Will murmured.

He was close behind, following as I moved through the cottage one last time. I grabbed my luggage and briefcase, and tugged on a new shirt. I'd change into a suit when I got to Texas. There was no sense wearing a tie all day if I didn't have to.

"What do you want?" I asked as I searched for my phone.

"You're leaving?" he asked.

Stopping, I stood in the middle of the kitchen, my arms spread wide. "What the fuck does it look like I'm doing?"

"How the hell should I know?" he asked. "Maybe you're moving in with Cupcake vonRebound."

"I have a meeting. Today. In Texas," I said. "She's not a rebound."

Will opened the refrigerator and helped himself to a bottle of water. "Right, so you're flying to Texas," he said. "Are you flying back here tonight? Or tomorrow?"

"No, I'm flying into Dulles," I said. I spied my phone between the couch cushions, and quickly toggled through the messages and notifications waiting for me. My mother wanted to hear about my weekend and hoped I'd been able to enjoy myself—*if she only knew*—and Marco said hello. I couldn't deal with a hello from Marco at this hour.

"You have access to a private jet, dude," he said. "You could fly into East Hampton and get your ass back here tonight if you wanted to."

If I do it once, I'll never stop.

I held up my phone, pointing to the endless stream of alerts that required attention. "Because I have a business to run and leaks to plug, and this isn't an opportune time to be away from the office," I said.

"You realize that we employ hundreds of people, right?" he asked, pointing the bottle at me. "And several of them are extremely capable individuals who would be thrilled to have a bit more work on their plates, right? And you're not only allowed but encouraged to delegate any of the fifty-seven thousand issues burning up your inbox, right?"

"This is *my* company, Will," I said, and then thought better of it. "Our company. Somehow I fell asleep at the wheel long enough to be compromised by Renner, see some of our best guys walk out, and watch a flawlessly planned mission go bad. Even if I want to give it up for a week with April, I can't do that right now. Do *you* get *that*?"

He nodded. "Of course," he said. "But it is *our* company, and I can spend a week in the D.C. office to get the house in order if you need a break."

"I was the one compromised. I'm going to deal with it," I said. "Now, unless you have any further sage advice, I've gotta hit the road."

"Take this from a guy who knows exactly how much a weekend in Montauk can change: don't take too long to get back here. Back to *her*," he clarified. "If she's one of the good ones, she'll slip through your fingers. Or start dating a douchelord just to grind your gears."

I pressed my fingertips to my temples. "Since when are you Team Cupcake?"

Will shot a *what the fuck is wrong with you?* scowl in my direction. "Of course I'm Team Cupcake." He rolled his eyes. "I was Team Titsy O'Silicone, too. I'm on your side, dude."

"I'm not sure which I find more troubling," I said, hefting my luggage and heading for the driveway. "That you let me date a woman who cheated on me with our primary competitor, or that you're capable of pulling these nicknames out of your ass."

Will opened the tailgate of my SUV and I loaded in my bags. "Probably the nicknames," he said, scratching the back of his neck. "It's proof that my brother-in-law is rubbing off on me."

CHAPTER THIRTEEN

TUESDAY

April: Hey. So…there are a lot of things I wish I'd said this morning, but I don't want to dump all of that into a text message. But I want you to know that I had the best weekend ever.

Jordan: Me too.

Jordan: It was amazing. You're amazing.

Jordan: I have to handle some business issues this week, but I promise I'll be back.

Jordan: Soon.

April: That's no problem at all as long as you agree to also seeing my pins.

Jordan: Ughhhhh

Jordan: Honey, please.

April: One acupuncture treatment isn't going to solve anything. If you had a wound, you wouldn't clean it once and wish it better. You'd clean it over and over, until it healed. This is exactly like that.

Jordan: You have mad skills. It's a problem.

April: …why would that be a problem?

Jordan: Because I need a goddamn nap after you work on me. That gets in the way of my desire to fuck you for hours on end.

April: But you're adorable when you're curled up with a blanket and napping.

Jordan: You get real bold when I'm 2000 miles away.

April: Did you type that with your scary voice?

Jordan: As a matter of fact, yes.

April: Mmmm. Love the scary voice.

April: (but you don't scare me)

Jordan: Did it make your panties fall off?

April: If you can believe it, yes. They're on the floor right now.

Jordan: Oh, honey…

———

WEDNESDAY

Jordan: Last night, I walked into an airport bookstore and browsed the romance section before my flight.

Jordan: Three different people asked me if I needed help finding something. Only two of them worked there. The other was a very concerned woman who thought I was lost, or a pervert.

April: Pervert. All the way.

Jordan: I blame you for this.

April: Blame away.

April: You know, you can always read on your tablet. Fewer judgey eyes. No uncomfortable public shopping experiences.

Jordan: I'll look into it.

Jordan: I'm in meetings the rest of the day. I'll catch up with you later.

April: No worries. I'm teaching a few classes tonight.

———

THURSDAY

Jordan: I know it's early but I just wanted to say good morning.

April: Good morning to you as well.

Jordan: I have another packed day today. Those business issues I mentioned, they're a big fucking mess right now. I don't think I can get back to Montauk this weekend.

April: My day is similarly packed. Cake catastrophes.

Jordan: I'd invite you to D.C., but I don't think anyone would leave Montauk for D.C. right now. My door is always open to you.

April: I'll keep that invitation in mind.

———

FRIDAY

Jordan: Good morning, honey.
Jordan: How are the cake catastrophes? Anything interesting on deck for this weekend's weddings?
Jordan: Is everything okay?
Jordan: Haven't heard from you in a bit.
Jordan: When you get a minute, just let me know that you're all right.

CHAPTER FOURTEEN

IT HAD ONLY BEEN THREE FULL DAYS SINCE LEAVING Montauk, but that time was inching along as if it were three decades. I was slammed with one highly critical meeting after another, and barely had a moment to shoot a few quick texts to April. I hadn't heard from her since yesterday morning, but I figured that was a product of one of her many professions.

Maybe she wasn't an avid texter. Maybe I needed to haul my ass back to Montauk if I wanted her attention. Not that I could fault her for that. She was worth the drive.

But I was left with a craving for April that no amount of work could silence. The time we'd spent together was short, but powerful. I missed her presence, her conversation, her humor, her body. I wanted a hit of that to diffuse the stress I'd packed on since returning to the office. Beating the shit out of the heavy bags at the gym was a sad substitute.

My teams were still running down leads on the bugs Renner planted in my apartment. It didn't appear they'd been in place long, but they were high-end models that could pull data from any device within a certain range. That meant my phone, tablet, and laptops had been compromised, and now we were scrambling to determine what Renner might have grabbed.

As if all of that weren't enough, it looked like Renner was going to submit a bid for the Riyadh deal, too. The odds were good that he'd been able to snag the presentation and terms I'd offered. With that leg up, we were certain to lose the deal. It was time to put all of these developments in front of Will, and get his take.

I tapped my phone to make the call, scowling when I realized April still hadn't replied to my early morning messages. Not only that, it had been more than twenty-four hours since receiving any response from her. She was too responsible to let her battery die and go unchecked for hours, and that left dueling concerns expanding in the pit of my belly. Either something was wrong or she was backing away from me.

"Jeremy," I called, hoping the senior analyst was within earshot. "*Jeremy*. Get in here."

I was scrolling through my texts—Mom felt it necessary to continue sending Marco's regards—when the tall, twentysomething hacker extraordinaire leaned against the doorframe. He nudged his glasses up his nose and took a sip from his iced coffee as he watched me. "What's up?" he asked.

I scribbled April's number on the notepad beside me, tore it off and thrust it toward Jeremy. "Run this down. I want to know the last time this number was active, and the towers it pinged."

He studied the paper for a moment, nodding. "You want a full download? Calls, texts, account info?"

That gave me pause. I tapped my pen against the desk as I thought. I had copious amounts of intelligence at my fingertips, but I wasn't about to start stalking April. I wasn't that guy. I simply wanted to confirm that she was all right. If, for some asinine reason, she didn't want me around, I'd respect that. I'd fight like hell, but I'd respect her while I did it.

"No." Jeremy's eyebrow arched, and it was clear that I didn't sound convinced. "No," I repeated, more certain now. "Last active and towers. That's all I want."

"Yeah, no problem," he replied, glancing at the number again. He pointed to the door. "You want this open?"

I shook my head. "Close it," I said, thinking back to my original intention of talking things over with Will. "I need to make a call."

When the door clicked shut, I tapped Will's contact information and waited for him to answer. He was busy preparing the logistics for an operation next week, and we didn't usually talk by phone unless there was an issue. In that sense, his response was unsurprising.

"What's wrong?" Will asked immediately.

"Should've killed Renner when I had the chance," I said. "He's bidding on the Riyadh deal."

"Let him," Will said. "There's nothing good about that deal. I hope he enjoys it. Just wait. He'll have a Stillhouse-branded keffiyeh soon enough."

I laughed, but there was no humor behind it. "It looks like he walked off with a shitload of our data."

"How in the fuck did this happen?" he asked. "I want to know how the actual fuck this occurred, Kaisall. What kind of toys does this motherfucker have that he can break through our systems, and what the fuck did he steal?"

I walked Will through the information that I had to this point. We couldn't do much about files that Renner already had, and we were altering tactics and targets as much as possible to prevent the original information from being actionable.

"There are more questions than answers," I said, tapping my pen against a stack of papers on my desk.

Will was silent for a moment, but then asked, "How long have you been sitting on these updates? A couple of hours or a couple of days?"

"Since yesterday morning," I said.

"Would've been nice to hear about this sooner."

"I know," I said, groaning. Of all the problems at hand, keeping Will updated shouldn't be one of them. That was all on me. "I didn't expect Renner's attempts to be successful. I figured he was working with basic bugs that accomplished little more than listening to me watch SportsCenter."

"Fuckin' Jocelyn," he said.

"Fuckin' Jocelyn," I agreed.

"What's the next move?" he asked.

I started to respond but there was a knock at my door. Jeremy poked his head in.

"Hang on, Halsted," I said, flipping on the speakerphone. Might as well invite Will into all of the problems now. "What do you have for me, Jeremy?"

He pointed at his notebook. "That mobile phone number last pinged near Montauk yesterday morning, but there hasn't been any tower activity since."

"Please tell me you haven't resorted to surveillance on vonRebound," Will murmured.

"It's not surveillance. Not exactly," I replied to Will. I pointed at Jeremy. "Anything else for me?"

"I know you didn't ask for this, but I checked the account information," Jeremy started, "and it's a burner phone. Looks like it was activated two weeks ago."

"*What*? Why would April have a burner?" I asked, mostly to myself.

I gripped the edge of my desk. It felt like my life —and business—were unraveling, and I couldn't do a damn thing to stop it.

"You can really pick 'em, Kaisall," Will said.

"Should I keep digging?" Jeremy asked.

"Yes," Will and I replied at once.

———

THE CONFERENCE ROOM WAS DARK, and the shadows were a welcomed reprieve from all the curious eyes. By now, my entire office knew of Jocelyn's duplicitousness and Renner's efforts at infiltrating the organization. A select few were busy tracking down April, but as the presentation underway seemed to indicate, that task was gaining complexity by the minute.

It seemed there was little to find.

"It appears that a signal jammer was in use here," Jeremy said, gesturing to the grainy photo on the screen. It was a blur of static, and I could make out the alleyway stairs leading to April's apartment only because I'd installed the camera to catch that exact angle. "Whenever she was within range, the jammer distorted the CCTV feeds. We couldn't pick anything up from the other CCTV feeds around town either. This was the clearest screen grab we could get." He laughed and tucked his hands into his trouser pockets. "Pretty sophisticated equipment. I'd love to get my hands on something like that."

What Jeremy wasn't saying was that the kind of technology that could interfere with every security camera April passed was beyond our expertise levels. We didn't have toys like that, and it wasn't for lack of innovation or investment. She was working with heavy-duty tools of the spycraft trade, and I'd taken her to bed without a second thought.

"What about the bakery? The apartment? Where's the paper trail on that?" I barked. "There has to be something."

The two other analysts seated around the table—not the ones who mentioned to Mom that they were investigating Marco, but the ones who could keep their mouths shut—stared at their laptop screens. It was a clear giveaway that they didn't want to speak up.

Jeremy cleared his throat and toggled to another slide. A photograph of a white-haired woman appeared on the screen, with an obituary beside it.

"We pulled the payroll records from the bakery," he said. "She's been on staff for three years, but the Social Security number is a dead end. It tracks back to a grandmother from Carefree, Arizona who died about ten years ago."

"Did you follow the money?" I asked. "Where are those payroll checks going?"

With a wince, Jeremy clicked over to the next slide. The backside of an endorsed check appeared. "All cashed by the bakery," he said. "Didn't even bother with a bank. Whoever she is, she's a pro."

Jeremy continued on, but I'd stopped listening. Breathing, too. The only thing I knew was that I knew *nothing*. Slapping my hands against the table, I stood and waved to Jeremy to end his report.

"That's enough," I said. I pocketed my phone and strode across the room. The conference room door bounced off the wall when I flung it open. "I'll be in the field for the rest of the day. Message me with any critical updates."

Storming through the office with the singular goal of getting the hell out of there, I collected a few kits from my office. I owed updates to Will, and my mother had left numerous messages in need of my response, but all of that had to wait. I was getting to the bottom of this.

CHAPTER FIFTEEN

"THIS IS FUCKING ABSURD," I MUMBLED TO MYSELF.

I'd had several hours' drive to talk myself out of this endeavor but when I arrived in the alley behind the bakery, I was as determined as ever. I had a strong idea what I was going to find before I started picking the loft apartment's lock, but that didn't stop me either.

It was as if I needed to prove to myself that I wasn't susceptible to this kind of manipulation. I could tolerate Jocelyn hooking up with Renner but I couldn't reconcile falling for a woman in possession of better spy gadgets than my shop. This was *my* game, and I wasn't prepared to admit that I'd been played until I could fill my hands with the truth and grind it all to dust.

A small, selfish part of me was still hoping that the version of April I'd known was real, and everything I'd experienced with her was real, too.

But reality came at me hard when the lock clicked

open and emptiness greeted me. The apartment that was once charmingly cluttered was now dim and vacant. Gone were the sun-bleached curtains and old trunks, the stacks of worn paperback books, the mismatched bedside tables. It was all gone.

I stepped inside, determined to touch the absence of her and bring it into my consciousness. I let my fingers graze the windowsills and walls, tracing the faint discolorations where artwork once hung. The tiny kitchen was scrubbed clean and the hanging fruit basket was already home to a spider web. Only the lobster magnet remained on the refrigerator, with "Montauk" scrawled on the shell. I plucked it off, turning it over in my palm as if it could reveal all of April's secrets.

Humid summer air moved over me as it raced to escape the confined space, and with it went my hope. I couldn't pretend there was any explanation other than the one dead ahead. April wasn't a sweet, sexy, silly woman who'd captured my heart in the crash of a wave. She wasn't a challenge, a mystery to uncover and explore.

April was a cover, and nothing more.

CHAPTER SIXTEEN

AFTER MY INJURY, ONE OF THE PHYSICAL THERAPISTS at Walter Reed encouraged me to secure a handicapped parking permit. He said I didn't have to use it every day, but it would be helpful when I was experiencing discomfort. I'd politely suggested he choke on my scrotum.

That conversation always came to mind when I was hiking through snow and ice, or when I'd pushed too hard in the gym, or after a there-and-back-again drive to Montauk. Hauling my ass across the parking garage buried beneath my apartment building—at three in the fucking morning, no less—was one throbbing reminder of my problems after another.

I was wide awake, hopped up on my outrage and ready to pound the shit out of something or drink myself into a dreamless sleep. Maybe both.

My leg ached as I shuffled down the hallway to my apartment, and my head and heart were a mess. I wanted to wallow in that, to spend a long time grabbing onto my self-pity and clutching it tight. I was prepared to do that, too, but when I stepped into my apartment, something was *off*. I couldn't bring words to that sensation, but only knew that the stillness in my space had been disturbed.

Adrenaline quickly piqued my senses. I carefully brought my hand to the small of my back, drawing a shallow breath as my fingers curled around the gun stowed there. I had the benefit of living in an open-plan apartment with a limited number of spots for intruders to hide out, but that didn't put me at ease. Given the shit storms I'd been contending with in recent weeks, I could be dealing with a common burglar, a hit man, a radicalized band of my mother's former online dating matches, or a new faction of the global war on terror.

It was anyone's guess.

I stepped away from the door, blinking into the darkness brightened only by the Capitol Hill lights in the distance, my steps soundless on the hardwood. The whir of the air conditioner drowned out everything but the rush of blood in my head. If I could cross the room and switch off the fan, I'd have a better chance of sniffing out the breach.

I didn't make it five steps before feeling a breath on the back of my neck and the cool sharpness of a knife at my throat.

"Hello, Jordan," the intruder whispered. That

voice. I *knew* that voice. "You did say the door was always open for me."

I knew that incense-and-herbs scent, too. It was stamped on my fucking soul.

"Drop the gun," April said. "I don't want to hurt you."

"Good fucking luck, honey," I murmured, hooking my leg around hers and knocking her off her feet. I'd expected the knife to clatter to the ground when she tumbled backward, but that was a basic error and it seemed she wasn't a basic warrior.

"You need to hear what I have to say, Jordan," she said as we regarded each other, weapons drawn. "Put the gun down."

"You think I need this?" I asked, waving my sidearm in her direction as we circled the kitchen island. "I can kill you with a paperclip and make it look like an accident."

She tipped the blade, and the sharp edge glimmered in the low light. It was a French-made Glauca B1, a brutal multi-tasker with the strength to break windows. It was the MacGyver of military knives, the weapon of choice for certified bad ass motherfuckers.

I had four of them.

"Who the fuck are you?" I asked, advancing on her.

"It was never meant to go down like this," she said. "I wasn't even supposed to talk to you."

She leapt over the sofa and skirted the coffee table to gain some space, but I didn't let her have it for long.

I followed, kicking and shoving the furniture until I had an obstacle course of destruction behind me and April backed into a corner. Unless she was capable of climbing walls—I wasn't putting anything past her—I was finally gaining an advantage in this game.

"I asked you a question," I said, aiming the gun straight at her. The bitter wrongness of this churned in my belly. "Who the fuck are you?"

She was flat against the wall now, and unless she was jumping out the window, I had her where I wanted her. For the briefest of moments, her eyes lost their trained focus as she realized the trap.

"I'm Israeli Mossad and CIA," she said. "But I need you to listen—"

I dived forward, growling as I pinned my forearm to her neck. She twisted beneath my hold as her oxygen supply waned, and the knife scored my flank. It wasn't a lethal wound but that didn't mean it hurt any less.

"The CI-fucking-A? Are you *fucking* serious?" I yelled, attempting to wrestle the blade from her grip. She was strong, and got in several more cuts in the process. That only ramped up my rage, and once I had it, I drove the knife into the wall a full foot above her reach. "And you fucking stabbed me?"

"Would you just listen to me?" she seethed.

I couldn't. I couldn't listen. I couldn't even look at her.

April seized that glimmer of vulnerability to draw both knees up and slam her heels into my chest. That move knocked the wind out of as me as I fell to the ground. I knew the kick well, and I knew it was intended to collapse a lung when executed perfectly. I figured this was how it would end. That she'd leave me there, gasping and bleeding, or maybe put me out of my misery altogether and close off whichever operation she was running.

But instead of doing that, April knelt beside me and brushed my hair off my forehead. It was just like that morning on the beach, but I couldn't tolerate the memory right now.

"It's awful, I know," she said softly. "Find a breath, tough guy. It's in there." She pressed her ear to either side of my chest, nodding as she sat up. "You're going to listen to me while you try to catch your breath."

"Go the fuck away," I wheezed.

"I left the covert services six years ago," she started, drawing my shirt up to inspect the wounds along my ribs. She frowned at them, but didn't look concerned. "It wasn't engaging for me anymore. I wanted to have interests and experiences that were my own, and not part of a cover."

"Oh, yeah," I replied, my voice hoarse and the words coming in jagged, pathetic gasps. "Kind of like how you're the friendly neighborhood acupuncturist who happens to be on hand the second I wipe out on my board? Is that the type of experience you're looking for?"

She folded her arms over her chest and shook her head. "I've picked up a few gigs from the CIA and private contractors, yeah," she said. "But only because the money is good and it's never more than light surveillance work. A little sneak-and-peek action." She tossed up her hands. "I wasn't supposed to interact with you. I was only to confirm your location. That's all Renner wanted."

Despite the burn in my chest, I sat up and pushed to my feet. I couldn't take another hit from Toby fucking Renner while flat on my ass. "Great, so you threw in the fuck for free."

April was on my heels in an instant, following me into the kitchen as I found a dishtowel to blot my wounds. She ripped it from my hands and applied the pressure herself. "Don't you ever speak to me that way again," she said, low and lethal. "*I* took you to bed. Not the spy. Not the soldier."

I stared into her eyes, and the forces of anger and affection battled for supremacy. My brain told me to show her the door, but my gut wasn't fully committed to that plan. One of them was right, but I didn't know which.

"I didn't give Renner any information about you," she said, her eyes blazing. "I wasn't on the beach as surveillance. I didn't realize it was you until it was too late, and after that moment, I was done. The only intel he got from me was to confirm that you were in Montauk."

"Great," I repeated. "Get in line behind the rest of the motherfuckers who've betrayed me, April." As her name passed over my lips, I stifled a groan. "If that's your name, of course."

The dishtowel ground into the wound and I gritted my teeth to keep from yelping. "My name *is* April," she said. "I didn't lie to you."

I broke away from her then, unable to keep up this ruse. "You were hired to track me. You failed to mention any of that." Stepping toward the bedroom, I scowled over my shoulder. "You're no friend of mine, lady. Show yourself out."

I didn't spare her a second look, instead discarding my bloodied shirt in the hamper and locating the first aid kit in my bathroom. As expected, the lacerations weren't life-threatening, and were adequately patched with wound glue and Steri strips. The mirror over the sink reflected a haggard man who'd fought and lost one too many fights. I flipped him off, and washed down several Advil with a handful of tap water.

I was ready for that dreamless sleep I'd pondered before finding myself on the receiving end of a zero dark attack, but April was waiting for me in the bedroom. She was staring out the window at the Capitol Hill skyline, and balancing on one foot in a modified tree pose. I only knew the name because I'd previously accused her of standing like a flamingo, and found myself thoroughly corrected. Her black-on-black attire was a sharp contrast to the bright white walls.

I started to object to her continued presence, but she moved away from the window, her steps slow and sure at the off-chance I wanted to go another round. Stopping in front of me, she brought her hands to my biceps.

There was a second where I thought about twisting those hands away and pinning them behind her back. Slamming her up against the wall. Pushing her around. Tossing her to the bed. Whether I'd fuck her or fight her wasn't clear.

"We need to talk about Venezuela, Jordan."

CHAPTER SEVENTEEN

MY ANGER AND FRUSTRATION OFTEN CAME WITH A side of shouting, but those who knew me best recognized that when I'd climbed every level of outrage and tripped over into blind rage, the yelling transformed into near silence.

"What the fuck did you just say?"

It was little more than a whisper but I was certain April heard every word.

She squeezed my upper arms and stared at me, steady and unyielding. Those espresso eyes, they took me right back to every time she'd ordered me onto her table or vibrated beneath me or shared—*fuck. No.* It was bullshit, all of it, and I couldn't fall prey to rose gold memories.

"If you have something to tell me, this is your moment, April," I said, shaking out of her hold. "You're long past the right to my patience."

Nodding, she started pacing the length of my

bedroom. I hated that seeing her here stirred up emotions that didn't match the circumstances. I didn't want to relax into the cadence of her voice or admire the way her braid swung between her shoulder blades. I didn't want any of her, and I was furious enough to swallow that lie.

"The CIA has been keeping an eye on Renner," she started. "They noticed he'd hired me, and one of my old handlers paid me a visit. It seems Renner's out of money, and on the verge of folding."

I chuckled at that. *Good fucking riddance to him.* "Maybe he should cut back on the swag spending," I said. "All those polo shirts must add up."

April stopped pacing and glowered at me, as if she recognized my comment as low and petty. It was, and she probably understood that. She wasn't a stranger to the intelligence community.

"She didn't tell me much, but my handler shared that Renner is losing clients," she continued. "He's doing everything to undercut his competitors, which is why he ordered surveillance on you. Based on everything I've seen, he can't keep up with your shop, Jordan. He's desperate."

"This isn't the time to tell me what a bang-up job I'm doing," I snapped. "Get to the point, or get the fuck out."

April watched me for a beat, and a sigh slipped from her lips. I knew that reaction. She wanted a different response from me, and she was disappointed that she didn't get it.

You're not getting anything. Not tonight.

"The CIA has reason to believe—but no actionable proof—he's resorted to illegal arms dealing to cover his expenses," she continued. "That's what caught most of their interest, and they were tracking him in Venezuela. He slipped through their fingers before they could draw him out in the weapons exchange. They don't know what went wrong, but I don't think they had the right assets in place and they're—"

"You want to know what went wrong?" I roared. Only the federal government could fuck things up forty ways to Friday. "I can tell you what went wrong. There's a three-hundred-page briefing book on my desk with a detailed analysis of *what went wrong.*"

I reached for my phone to wake up everyone at the Agency. They needed to hear how my rescue mission went sour because they were courting a cum-guzzling bastard into selling them weapons, only for that same bastard to turn around and resell those weapons to a militant group with a taste for human trafficking.

I would've succeeded, but April climbed across the bed and snatched it away. "Did you know Renner was in Venezuela all along?" she asked.

"Of course not. We don't engage when we can't control the entire operation," I said. "But after debriefing the team that was on the ground, we determined the last-minute arms deal set off the chain of events that closed every window we had for executing the rescue." I pointed to the device she was holding. "I'd like to inform my partner that he's now allowed to hunt Renner, and bring me his head on a spear. You don't need to be here for that."

April chucked a pillow at me. "I came here because I care about you, but you *must* know how dangerous it is for me to reveal classified information," she said. "If you're certain you don't want this— or me—I'll leave."

Don't go.

It was the first thought in my head, and she must've been able to see it all over my expression.

She reached into her pocket and produced a phone —not mine, not the one I'd seen in her apartment last weekend either—and tossed it to the middle of the bed. "There's more. Take a look," she said. "By the way, no one knows where Renner is right now. His passport was flagged in Dubai, but he's been off the radar for the past two days."

"I have a decent idea where he's headed," I murmured. Curious, I picked up the device from where it landed on the duvet and swiped it to life. Images of overdue invoices, bank statements, and client work orders confirmed April's comments, but then I came upon a hand-scrawled list of names. I turned the screen toward her. "Where did you get this?"

"I broke into his office last night." She shrugged like it was no big deal, and I still couldn't believe I'd surrendered my soul to a spy. "If you thought my apartment had a loosey-goosey approach to security, you should've seen the Stillhouse facility."

"Too soon, April. Too fucking soon," I muttered. "Why does Renner have these names?"

She shook her head. "My handler tracked them all back to a small outfit specializing in security services for fancy gated communities along the Delmarva Peninsula. Coastal Elite Securities." Another head shake. "It's not clear what Renner wants with that information, or its relevance."

I laughed out loud. "I must be doing something right," I said, surveying the list of my most effective covert operatives again.

Protecting their identities was essential to the safety of our work as well as their private lives and families, and building several layers of shell corporations between the organization's public face and their paychecks was the primary firewall. The vast, unregulated expanse of foreign surveillance programming meant that anyone could access personal information, and use that information to target and expose the men and women I employed.

Not on my watch.

"What does that mean?" April asked. "Do you know something about this list?"

Crossing my arms, I leaned against the closet door as I studied her. I wasn't sure I recognized the woman in front of me. I knew those lips, those eyes, that dark braid, but I knew the easygoing beach chick who liked historical romances and kitchen sink salads. The spy —the one who kicked my ass without a hair sliding out of place—wasn't the one who carved a spot for herself in my heart.

"I do," I said, "and one week ago, I would've told you. I would've shared anything and everything with you, but then you gave me a burner phone number and dropped off the grid before breaking into my apartment and *stabbing the shit out of me*." I shook my head. The sting of being the subject of April's deception didn't soothe quickly, regardless of the reason. "Sorry, sweetheart, but I can't read you in just yet."

April set my phone on the bedside table and approached me, her hands held out. "I had to come here. I had to tell you," she whispered. "Even if it meant disappearing for a while. Even if it meant hurting you. Even if it meant hurting myself. I couldn't let you go without the truth."

She gazed up at me with eyes like a moonless night, and my defenses started crumbling.

"You promised you'd come back to me when your affairs were in order," she continued. "I felt it was only right to extend you the same courtesy."

I didn't refuse her this time, instead allowing her fingertips to travel over my chest and arms.

"What are you going to do?" she asked, tracing the frog skeleton tattoo on my shoulder.

Her eyes were cast down, and I couldn't read her expression. I was left gazing at the sweep of her dark eyelashes and wondering how I'd find an answer to her question.

I'm going to take Renner down and tear apart what's left of his shop.

I'm going to lose myself in your embrace and pretend there's a way for us to move forward.

I'm going to strip you naked and torment your body for a good long while.

I'm going to watch you leave, and then spend the rest of my days hating myself for letting you go.

"I'm going to call my partner, and then take a drive down to Virginia," I said finally. "He's gonna want to burn Langley down, but I'm sure we'll mention where they might find Renner. They also need a primer on how their assets dicked-over a major rescue operation."

"That can wait until the morning," she said. "It's late."

"You of all people should know there's no rest for spies," I argued.

April's eyelashes fluttered against her cheeks and she nodded, her palms flat on my chest. It wasn't what she'd wanted to hear, and it wasn't what I'd wanted to say.

"I'm sorry about stabbing you," April said after several silent minutes. "And the solar plexus strike. I didn't need to do that, but I can't remember the last time someone relieved me of my weapon and lived to tell about it."

"It seems we're more alike than we'd suspected," I said. "But you already knew that, didn't you?"

She dropped her forehead to my bare chest. The

contact was light, but it sent my entire body into over-drive. My breath whooshed out in a startled, needy gasp. My skin pebbled at her nearness. My vital organs were slamming against muscle and bone, unde-cided whether they were alive with arousal or protecting themselves in advance of another battle.

"I'm sorry about misleading you," she whispered. "I wanted to tell you the truth so many times. I've never wanted to do that before. Not once. Not for anyone. Only you, Jordan."

That took the fight right out of me, and though it ran contrary to every shred of reason, I wrapped my arms around her waist and yanked her close.

"Do you remember that morning at your cottage?" she asked. My chin bobbed against the crown of her head. "I was going to tell you everything. I've never broken my cover before, but I was going to do it for you."

"You must've been a damn good spy," I murmured into her hair. "You still are."

"I'm going to stick with the cakes and bodywork. The Montauk gossip mill is plenty of excitement for me," she said, nuzzling her face into my chest.

Come closer. I fucking missed you, honey.

"But you left Montauk," I said.

April shook her head and then slipped away from me to untie her boots. She yanked them off, shoved her socks in each, and then loosened her braid. "I had to clear out, yeah," she said. "I had to go back to my old handler, and make sure the CIA didn't think your shop was colluding with Renner. It's unlikely, but why else would he hire me to track you?"

"Because he's a cum-guzzling weasel," I said.

"I'm not arguing with that," she said, returning to my arms. "Jordan, you have to know that if any part of this went off the rails—including you suggesting that I'd shared classified intel regarding an ongoing CIA operation—I had to vanish." Her expression turned pained. "If everything settles down, I'll go back to Montauk soon. I liked it there. It was finally starting to feel like home, and I want it to be home again."

Her hands dropped to my belt, and my jeans were on the ground seconds later. I reciprocated, peeling her close-fitting layers off and delighting in her smooth skin. "What about your Social Security number, and the grandmother from Arizona?"

April shot me an amused glance. "Retired spies like to keep a low profile," she said. "Some creative bookkeeping makes that easier." She pulled the duvet back and then gestured to the bed. "Which side do you sleep on?"

A wiser, more pragmatic version of me would've recounted her betrayals and penchant for knife fighting, and tossed her out on her ass.

This intensely flawed and foolish version of me pulled her body against mine and kissed her hard enough to steal her breath. I took her to bed and loved her like I wanted to destroy her.

There were no promises, no declarations, no words beyond the most basic expressions of need and assent, but our bodies hadn't forgotten how to say everything we couldn't.

CHAPTER EIGHTEEN

"Special Agent Severino," Will called, tipping his chin up in greeting when the other man stepped inside the Waffle House.

We were seated at a table in the far corner, Will with his baseball cap pulled low and his arms crossed over his chest, and me with a memory card that would demolish Toby Renner's business and liberty tucked in my back pocket.

"It's Sunday morning, Halsted," the agent replied. He jerked the empty chair away from the table and sat, his exaggerated exhale a sure sign that we'd fucked up his weekend. *Good.* "What the hell is going on? I'm missing my kid's swim meet for this shit."

Will gestured to the carafe of coffee. "How do you take it, Mike?" He reached for the mug stationed on the top corner of the agent's placemat and filled it with steaming liquid. "Black? Milk and sugar? Up the ass or all over your face?"

"William," I scolded, sending him a scowl of faux disapproval across the table before turning back to Severino. "I apologize for my partner. He's the savage in this relationship. What he was trying to say is this: we have a bit of information that may be of interest to you."

Mike rocked back in his chair and offered a bitter grimace. "That's pretty fucking unlikely."

Will set the mug in front of the agent, hot coffee sloshing over the sides in the process. "How long has it been since you had eyes on Toby Renner?" he asked, tapping the face of his watch. "It's only been fifteen minutes since I pulled his coordinates, but you've probably got that covered."

The agent turned to me, blinking. "If this is a game, I'll make it my mission to guarantee neither of you ever get another Department of Defense contract."

"This must be difficult for you," I said. "It can't be every day that you misplace a treasonous black-market arms dealer."

"Or do you have so many that you can't keep up with all of them?" Will asked.

"Jesus Christ," Severino muttered as he reached for his coffee. He loaded it up with sugar and cream, and clanked his spoon around the mug while he stirred. "Where the fuck are you people getting your information? Why are you even involved with Stillwater's operations?"

Will snorted. "What aren't we involved with?" he asked.

I knocked my knuckles on the tabletop, drawing Severino's attention back to me. "We have his location, his comms, his contacts. We have satellite footage of him exchanging weapons for cash on three different continents, and we have the pertinents of his next sale," I said. "I would encourage you to take this conversation seriously, Special Agent."

Severino lifted the mug to his lips and sipped, but his gaze was mapping the off-ramp diner. "The type of conversation you're starting requires a more secure location," he said under his breath. "We have a site about twenty minutes from here if—"

"Nope," Will interjected. "We're here for the waffles, man."

"Waffles, and a terabyte of data that might make your next steps a whole lot simpler," I added.

"But if you don't want that," Will started, his palms held out as he shrugged, "we have the operatives in place to handle this affair for you. You know, before it turns into a widespread intelligence failure."

The agent tapped the spoon against the lip of his mug for a solid minute, and I was amazed Will didn't stab him in the heart with it during that time. "What are you looking to get out of this?" he asked, gesturing between us with the offending spoon. "Clearly, you're not offering this information from the goodness of your hearts. There must be something you need."

Will dropped his forearms to the tabletop and leaned forward. "Not much, really," he said easily. "Just a warship."

I LACED my fingers together and stretched my arms over my head, forcing a loud pop from my neck in the process. Will was busy chasing the last crumbs of waffle around his plate and paid no attention while I shook the tension from my joints.

"Are you heading back to Boston this afternoon?" I asked.

He murmured in agreement as he chewed. "That private jet situation isn't a difficult adjustment," he said as he rubbed a paper napkin over his lips. "Can we work out a custody agreement? You get the jet one month, I get it the next."

"Where the fuck do you even go that you'd need a jet?" I asked.

He waved at the diner's interior. "I fly to Virginia to fix the CIA's intel problems for them," he replied. "Just curious, though. Where'd we get that tip about Renner being behind the arms deal in Venezuela? We probably wouldn't have dug into that side of the surveillance footage without it."

"Cupcake," I mumbled as I reached for my coffee.

"Cupcake?" he repeated. "Cupcake vonRebound?"

I met his eyes but didn't respond until I'd drained the coffee. "Yeah," I said finally. "Turns out she has a history in the covert services. Mossad. CIA. Private contracting." I wrapped my hands around the empty mug, nodding. "Renner hired her to track me. Like any decent spy, she stole intel from his office and shared classified material. She divulged all of this information to me after breaking into my apartment and stabbing me several times."

He gazed at me for several long beats, his features expressionless. Then, he tugged his cap off and dragged his fingers through his hair. "You really know how to pick them, Kaisall," he said, wagging the cap in my direction. "Where's Cupcake now?"

On an exhale, I shook my head. "Don't know," I said. Those words poked an ache behind my breastbone, and not only from the ugly bruises left by the impact of April's heels on my chest. "She left after providing the leads on Renner."

That wasn't the entire truth, but I had no desire to share the details of my pre-dawn hours in bed with April. It'd been rough and punishing, and we'd fallen asleep in a tangled pile of limbs and linens. When I woke hours later, April—and her Glauca B1—was gone. My apartment was a wreckage of broken furniture and home goods, and a trail of blood on the hardwood floors, walls, and linens charted our movements.

"*Don't know* meaning she has another contract?" Will asked. "Or meaning the era of Cupcake has ended?"

I narrowed my eyes at him. "I was her mark," I said with an uncomfortable laugh. "How can the era of Cupcake continue?"

"Ahhh," he replied, brushing aside my objection. "You said it yourself. She stole information from Renner and wherever-the-fuck-else to help us, and then kicked your ass. You keep that kind of chick around for the long haul. Marry her."

"I'll take that under consideration," I said, pulling my phone from my pocket to avoid catching Will's eyes. I was too raw to continue discussing this, and didn't have room for suggestions of marriage, no matter how mild.

"Seeing as we've gotten to the bottom of our crises, and the Navy will be supporting our next rescue attempt in Venezuela, it's time for you to take some time off," Will said. He held up his hand as I started to object. "I know how you are. I know you can't unplug completely, and I'm not asking that."

"When did you turn into such a tenderhearted bastard?" I asked.

He flipped me off. "Get your ass back to Montauk, and don't make me call in Mama Trish for backup."

CHAPTER NINETEEN

IT TOOK A FULL WEEK BEFORE I WAS READY TO LEAVE the office for more than a few hours, but when I was, I didn't think twice about going.

The drive to Montauk was loaded with memories of my recent journeys, and I was quick to fill the miles with phone calls as not to spend the time reexamining the highs and lows I'd experienced with April.

Clients in need of hand-holding and reassurance—mostly billionaires and politicians—were on the top of my list. They always wanted to hear that they were my first priority, and I never suggested otherwise.

Those in the know—Washington insiders, the intelligence community, SEAL Team veterans—knew something hadn't been right in my shop, and they were hungry for details. For them, I had a simple story of stumbling across information that belonged in the CIA's hands and seeing that it got there.

That left my inner circle—Will, Jeremy, and my

mother—and they required an update on my schedule for the coming weeks. The first two were quick calls, and I appreciated the fuck out of Will and Jeremy's ability to keep the conversation focused on business.

My mother had no such ability.

"Redtop Securities, this is Trish," she chirped.

"Hey, Mom," I said. "I know you've been trying to get a hold of me—"

"What a darn understatement," she interrupted. "But I understand things have been busy around the office."

"Also an understatement," I replied. "There were a few hiccups, but now we're back on track. I'm actually taking some time away from D.C. I'm heading out to the Hamptons now. I've delegated several pitch meetings so there's no need to cancel anything. I don't want any new clients calendared until I have a chance to review and decide who should take the meeting. I want my schedule blocked for the next two weeks."

She murmured in agreement as her fingers clattered against the keyboard. "Done and done," she said. "Is there anything you'd like to tell me?"

I didn't know how to answer that. "What do you mean?" I asked.

"You haven't spent more than a couple of days at the shore in years, and now you're going back for an extended stay," she said. "This makes me think you met someone."

"There is someone," I confessed. "But it's complicated. Really complicated."

"Well," she said, pausing to sip her soda. "I know how difficult that is."

I narrowed my eyes and scowled at the road ahead. "Is there anything you'd like to tell me?" I asked.

"I've decided that I've had my fill of the dating scene. I understand it makes you uncomfortable that I'm single and ready to mingle, and I don't want that," she said.

There was no right answer here. "Mom, no," I said with a groan. "Listen. If you want to get out there and meet some guys, I'll support your choices. I don't want you basing this decision on me. You're allowed to mingle, and I'm sorry that I've made you feel badly about mingling."

"No, this is what I want," she said, resolute. "I've had a lot of fun and quite a few pleasurable experiences—"

"Let me stop you right there," I interrupted. There was definitely a vein popping out of my forehead right now. "Nope, we do not need to have a conversation about *experiences*. Not at all."

Her nails tapped against her soda can for a long beat before she continued. "I hope you can accept that I'm not interested in marriage either."

"Accept it?" I asked, incredulous. "What are you talking about? It's not for me to accept or reject. Like I said, I'll respect your choices regardless of whether you're in a serious relationship, casually dating, or engaging in some other"—I actually choked on my words—"arrangement. Do what makes you happy, Mom. You deserve it."

"I appreciate that, Jordan. Thank you, sweetie," she said. "You're right about doing what makes me happy. I think you'd like Marco."

"Oh, really?" I grumbled.

"Of course," she replied. "He's moving in with me next week, and I can't wait for you to meet him."

"Oh, fuck me, Moses," I said under my breath.

CHAPTER TWENTY

MY FIRST WEEK IN MONTAUK WAS STRANGE FOR MANY reasons. The summer, at least as it pertained to vacationers and beachgoers, was over. The town was settling back into its sleepy ways, and that brought a degree of quiet I hadn't anticipated. I missed the frenetic pace of the Beltway and my office, and often considered abandoning this adventure and returning home. But then I found a balance of working, swimming, and sleeping that felt manageable. Comfortable, even.

I didn't look for April once.

That wasn't completely accurate. I took pains to avoid passing the bakery and local yoga studio, but I couldn't stay away from the place where it all started. Every morning, I paddled out to the spot where I'd sat on my board weeks ago. I harbored no illusions about riding the waves now, but I hoped to see the pretty dark-haired girl as she searched for seashells.

She never crossed my path, and after that first week, I wasn't certain she'd come back to Montauk. I'd held up my end of the bargain by turning over the intel without implicating her in any way, and it should've been safe for her to return to life as she'd known it. She deserved the life she'd built here.

When my second week in Montauk rolled around, I was ready to go after her again.

My first stop was the bakery. I spent an extended amount of time surveying the goods on display while sneaking glances at the cake decorating work station, but didn't see April. I bought a huge box of pastries, and hoped it came with a side of information.

"Is April in today?" I asked the cashier. "I was thinking about ordering something special, and I know she's the best when it comes to fondant roses. My mother's birthday is coming up."

The cashier wiped her hands on her apron and shook her head. "No, April had a family emergency," she said. "Such a sweetheart, that one. She's back on the schedule next week, and not a minute too soon. Everyone loves her work." She pulled a notebook from behind the counter and pointed at me with her pencil. "Do you want to leave your name and number? She can give you a call."

I hefted the bakery box and moved toward the door. The promise of her nearness—even if it was days away—activated corners of my heart that had gone dormant. "I'll check back," I said. "Thank you."

With the pastries abandoned on the passenger seat

of my SUV, I marched through the village and toward the yoga studio. The class schedule was posted on the storefront window, but I couldn't find April's name listed there.

That left only the loft apartment, and I climbed each step with a percolating sense of nervous hope. I wanted her to be there more than anything, but I had no idea what I'd say or do if she was. At the top of the staircase, I peered inside but found no evidence of her return.

I took my time getting home. I followed the coast road for miles, taking in the towns and villages as I worked through my disappointment. I convinced myself it was temporary, that I'd find April in due time, that my life had meaning and purpose even if it didn't have her.

The sun was sinking toward the horizon when I pulled into the cottage's gravel driveway. The long-forgotten bakery box in hand, I made my way inside with the singular goal of kicking back on the porch for the next few hours. The first stop was the refrigerator, and I hooked my fingers around the necks of two beer bottles. This felt like the right time to get good and drunk.

"You should really lock your doors."

I froze, blinking at the contents of the refrigerator while the sound of her voice sent my thoughts skittering away from me. Pivoting, I slammed the refrigerator shut to find April curled up with a book on my sofa.

April.

On my sofa.

In my house.

"I doubt that would stop you," I said. There was more ice in my voice than I'd intended. If April noticed, her slightly arched eyebrow was the only reaction.

She smiled and set the book down. "You're probably right about that." Pointing at the bottles I was holding, she asked, "Is one of those for me?"

April, honey.

"That depends," I replied, my feet still nailed to the kitchen floor as my gut churned with longing. "Where've you been?"

"Chicago," April said with a shrug. "Tali's guest bedroom never fails to sort out my problems." Her voice trailed off as she stood and walked toward me. She was wearing a dress, and at some point in the future—when I had the brain cells necessary to think beyond my most primitive needs and wants—I'd remember how amazing she looked. How the fabric swirled around her thighs and the v-neck skimmed her breasts. *So luscious.*

"Are you staying?" I couldn't shake the sharp tone from my words, even if I was a breath away from dropping to the floor and worshiping at her feet.

Come here, honey.

"Well..." She was leaning against the countertop, just within reach, and something shifted inside me. It could've been my cold, cynical heart thawing or the knots in my neck loosening, and both were reasonable explanations. But there was more to it. "I've already taken a few drawers and most of the closet space. I hope you don't mind."

Take everything. Take it all. Take me.

"Get the fuck over here," I ordered, my words rushing out in a pant. I set the beers on the countertop and caught a fistful of her dress, tugging her into my arms. "I love you."

"I know," she said, her lips on my jaw. "You came back for me, just like you'd promised. Even after everything I—"

"Shut up," I said, driving my fingers through her hair. My lips met hers—sweet, sweet honey—and my body ached for her. That was it. I was making room for her, moving around my stiff ways and rusty edges, and possessing her. "Just shut up and tell me you love me, too."

Her shoulders rocked with quiet laughter. "Should I shut up?" she asked, her words bubbling over with laughter. "Or should I tell you I love you?"

I hooked an arm under her backside, and her legs twined around my waist. "Shut up about everything else and tell me how much you love me," I said as I charged for the bedroom.

"I love you so much that I won't point out you're seriously favoring your left leg and clearly need some time on my table," April said when I set her on the blue quilt. "You know me. You know how much I want to look after that leg." Her eyes dropped and she licked her lips. "How much I want to look after you."

"I'll let you," I said. I pushed her back and tore her panties out from underneath her, grinning when her eyes widened. "Just promise you won't stab me again, honey."

EPILOGUE

ONE YEAR LATER

SHANNON NUDGED MY ELBOW. "What do you think they're talking about out there?" she asked, her gaze trained on Will and Jordan.

They were outside, near the dunes that separated the land from the shore, and engaged in a heated debate that involved emphatic gestures and vehement head shaking. If not for the full moon, they would've disappeared under the cover of darkness.

I murmured but didn't tear my eyes from the men. Or one man in particular. My tall, dark man with the panty-dropping voice.

"I think they're debating the proper way to build a snowman," I said, watching as Jordan motioned roundly only for Will to slash a hand in front of him.

"Maybe it's something about football. There's always something to argue about when it comes to football."

Shannon didn't respond, sipping her sparkling water as she watched our men. There hadn't been an announcement yet, but I was interpreting the lack of liquor in her life as an indication she and Will were expecting baby number three.

Abby was asleep upstairs, in the bedroom she called "mine, mine, mine." That little girl loved Montauk and the cottage Will and Shannon were renting this month. Jordan's mother, Trish, was busy rocking Annabelle to sleep on the back porch while reminiscing about babyhood with Marco. She took great pleasure in telling everyone that Jordan had been bigger as a newborn than seven-month-old Annabelle.

"Did Jordan say anything about their trip to the training facility?" Shannon asked.

Work was nearly complete on Redtop's expanded site, and Jordan and Will had inspected the progress on their way back from a series of meetings in Miami last week. After eight months of non-stop construction, the expansion project was finally winding down. And it wasn't a moment too soon. Though Jordan had worried about stepping away from D.C. and delegating day-to-day management to his deputy Jeremy, business was brisk. The fallout from the shuttering of Stillhouse left Redtop with many new clients, although Toby Renter's whereabouts remained a mystery.

The Agency didn't make a habit of publicizing the guest lists at their off-grid black site prisons.

"Some," I said. I tucked my feet beneath me as I resettled on the sofa. "Mostly complaints about Miami, and then some noise about wanting to double the size of the shooting range again."

Jordan traveled a fair amount, but the departures were what made the arrivals so sweet. We planned our reading around his schedule, and that meant we always had new books to discuss and amorous moments to role-play when he got home.

It was hard to believe it, but that's what we had. A *home*. After years of bouncing from one place to another, a new cover story for every city, it was amazing to have a place that was mine.

But it wasn't the oceanfront cottage or the Long Island location. It was Jordan.

The beach was wonderful and the hamlet of Montauk was storybook-perfect and everything I had here was a-freaking-mazing, but Jordan was the home I'd long craved. He was my rock, my anchor, my port in the storms of life—all of it, and then some.

And he wouldn't stop teasing me about stabbing him.

"That goddamn range," Shannon muttered. "They won't be happy until they have nineteen miles of unobstructed shooting range space." She turned to me abruptly. "I forgot to ask about your class schedule this week. Do you have anything basic that won't make me dizzy or irritable?"

I stifled a laugh and reached for my wineglass. Shannon and I had become close over the past year, and I'd learned her tolerance for yoga was lean. She preferred simple stretching and breathing, despite being a hard-core runner and spin enthusiast. "I have a beginner's class tomorrow afternoon," I said. "Four o'clock at the studio."

"Will it be packed with city folk and tourists?" she asked. "Not that I mind."

I cut a glance to Will and Jordan, and found them in the thick of their snowmen-and-football argument. They reveled in barking at each other. "Tourists hit up the morning classes," I said. "I see more locals in the afternoon."

She nudged me again. "They're probably debating something ridiculous, like how to build a bomb with an orange peel," she said, nodding toward the dunes. I had opinions about orange peel bomb-building but kept them to myself. Though Will and Shannon knew of my history as a covert operative, it wasn't information that I advertised. "I'm gonna break this up."

I followed Shannon down the stony path leading from the house to the beach. As we neared the men, I caught shards of their conversation but not enough to make sense of it.

"It's past your bedtime, commando," Shannon called.

Jordan pivoted as we approached, and he regarded me with the cool, confident gaze that still sucked me in like a force field.

"You have orders," Will said to Jordan. "Follow them."

Will and I passed each other on the path as we traded places. "What was that about?" I asked Jordan when we were alone.

He hooked his arm around my shoulders and urged me toward the shore. "Home?"

We walked through the sand as waves crashed nearby. Our place was a short distance from Will and Shannon's, and I could spot the twinkle lights bordering our porch. The cottage was now home to an addition because Jordan hated working from the kitchen table. We had a bit more elbow room, and tidy spaces for his office and my bodywork, and—

"Will you marry me?" he asked, his lips brushing over my ear.

"What?" I glanced at him, confused. "What did you say?"

Jordan shoved his hands into his pockets with a ragged exhale. "Well, that didn't come out right," he murmured. He held out a red ring box. It dawned on me that this was no spur-of-the-moment proposal. "Hold this. Stay right here. I have to go strangle Will."

"Is that what you were arguing about?" I asked, wrapping both hands around the box. Tears filled my eyes for no good reason. *I'm not going to cry. I'm not going to cry. Fuck, I'm crying.* "How to propose?"

He moved to kneel before me, but I reached out to stop him. My man wasn't meant for bended knee.

"Don't do that," I sob-yelled. "No kneeling. None of that. Stand up when you speak to me."

Jordan took my face in his hands and brushed my tears away. "April, honey. Why are you crying?" he asked softly.

Because I love you for always.

Because I don't need a ring or vows to be happy but I want my forever with you.

Because I anticipate every move but missed this one.

"It's all right if you don't want this. I'll survive," he said. He lifted a shoulder. "You can say no."

"Clever, aren't you?" I asked through a sniffle. "Did Will help you pick out the ring, too?"

He pressed his forehead to mine as he huffed out a laugh. "That savage? No. Don't you think I can manage on my own?"

I hesitated. Jordan was meticulous about many things. He was a sharply dressed man and his homes reflected that same style. But I'd once spent an hour explaining the difference between pendants and bib necklaces to him with little success. "You can, but—"

"Shannon helped me pick it out," he confessed.

I sucked in a breath. "You've been planning this since your trip to Boston?" I asked. *How the hell did he slip this one past me?* "That was months ago."

Jordan opened the box and plucked the ring from its seat. I watched, dumbfounded, as he dropped the box to the sand. "You're not the only one who can run a good covert op," he said, the ring's cool metal sliding over my skin. "Say yes, April."

I stared at it for a second, the stone winking in the moonlight, and then brought my arms around Jordan. I wanted his skin against mine, and I tugged his shirt from his belt. "Yes, because I love you for always," I said, sighing when my hands met the small of his back. "Yes, because I don't need a ring or vows to be happy but I want my forever with you." My legs went around his waist when he lifted me up. "Yes, because I know your moves, and I know that one means you're taking me home now."

"Right away, ma'am," Jordan said as he marched toward our cottage.

ACKNOWLEDGMENTS

Putting a book together and readying it for the public is a team effort, and I continue to be awed by the people who choose to call themselves members of Team Writer Lady.

My editor, Julia, deserves sainthood. She works miracles and puts up with drafts that resemble story spaghetti.

My left and right hands, Amanda and Robyn, continue to be the most supportive, patient, kind, salty, funny, amazing people out there. I'm thankful they tolerate my cyclical meltdowns and existential (but not really) crises.

My author friends, the ones who are always on hand to dole out an ass-kicking when I need it.

My pervy girls in The Walshery, you really are pervs. Don't change.

My husband, who only rolls his eyes a little bit when I come to bed at four in the morning after writing all night.

NEW FROM KATE CANTERBARY

Preservation

Book Seven in The Walsh Series
Coming May 23, 2017

Some things have to fall apart before they can be put back together.

Available for ebook preorder from all major ebook sellers.

NEW FROM KATE CANTERBARY

BEFORE GIRL

A sexy new standalone coming in 2017

She's the girl next door.
He's the guy who's loved her from afar.
They're in for an unexpected tumble into love.

She'll juggle your balls.
For Stella Allesandro, chaos is good. She's a rising
star at a leading sports publicity firm. She's known
throughout the industry as the jock whisperer—the
one who can tame the baddest of the bad boys in
professional sports without losing her signature
smile.

But Cal Hartshorn is an entirely different kind of
chaos.

He'll fix your broken heart.
This ex-Army Ranger and now-famous cardiothoracic
surgeon fails at nothing…except talking to a woman
he's adored from afar. Whether on the battlefield or
operating room, he's exacting, precise, and efficient,
but all of that crumbles when Stella is in sight.

Cal always knows—and gets—what he wants, and
now he wants all of her. His *forever* girl.

But Stella isn't convinced she's anyone's forever.

ALSO BY KATE CANTERBARY

Underneath It All – Matt and Lauren

The Space Between – Patrick and Andy

Necessary Restorations – Sam and Tiel

The Cornerstone – Shannon and Will

Restored — Sam and Tiel

The Spire — Erin and Nick

Preservation — Riley and…

Get exclusive sneak previews of upcoming releases through Kate's newsletter and private reader group, The Walsh Groupies, on Facebook.

You can also follow her on Twitter (lots of random commentary about shoes, food, and the Boy Assistant), Facebook (lots of peeks at the work in progress and books she's fangirling over), Instagram (lots of old homes, food and drink and drink and drink, the stray sexy men in suits, and the odd nature photo), Tumblr (lots of hot nakedness), Goodreads, and her website.

ABOUT KATE

Kate Canterbary doesn't have it all figured out, but this is what she knows for sure: spicy-ass salsa and tequila solve most problems, living on the ocean—Pacific or Atlantic—is the closest place to perfection, and writing smart, smutty stories is a better than any amount of chocolate. She started out reporting for an indie arts and entertainment newspaper back when people still read newspapers, and she has been writing and surreptitiously interviewing people—be careful sitting down next to her on an airplane—ever since. Kate lives on the water in New England with Mr. Canterbary and the Little Baby Canterbary, and when she isn't writing sexy architects, she's scheduling her days around the region's best food trucks.

You can find Kate on Twitter, Facebook, Instagram, Goodreads, and her website.